TIME FOR
ANDREW

MARY DOWNING HAHN is the author of more than a dozen books for young people, including the award-winning *Stepping on the Cracks*. She is a former children's librarian who lives in Columbia, Maryland, with her husband, Norm.

TIME FOR ANDREW

A Ghost Story

MARY DOWNING HAHN

AN AVON CAMELOT BOOK

AVON BOOKS
A division of
The Hearst Corporation
1350 Avenue of the Americas
New York, New York 10019

First Avon Camelot Printing: April 1995

CAMELOT TRADEMARK REG. U.S. PAT. OFF. AND IN OTHER COUNTRIES, MARCA REGISTRADA, HECHO EN U.S.A.

Printed in the U.S.A.

OPM 10 9 8 7 6 5 4 3

For all my friends in Missouri,
especially
Philip A. Sadler and Ophelia Gilbert,
who have contributed so much to so many.

A big thanks from all the birds who
migrate to Warrensburg every spring!

Chapter 1

"There it is." Dad slowed the car and pointed to a big brick house standing on a hill above the highway. From a distance, it looked empty, deserted, maybe even haunted.

"Oh, Ward," Mom whispered to my father, "it's in terrible shape. From what your aunt said, I thought —"

Dad glanced at me. "What do you mean, Nora? Just look at the woods and fields, the river, the hills. Drew will have a great time here. Just great. It's a boy's paradise."

Unfortunately, Dad's enthusiasm was lost on me. My idea of paradise would be part museum, part library, part amusement park, not a spooky old house in the country.

While Dad raved about the joys of hiking and bird-watching, I stared at the endless fields of corn gliding past the car window. I wanted to tell him I'd changed my mind, I'd go to camp after all, but it was too late. Everything was settled. My parents were going to France, and I was staying with Great-aunt Blythe. It had seemed like a good idea last spring, but now that I'd seen the house I wasn't so sure.

Although I hadn't opened my mouth, Dad guessed what I was thinking. "You could be at Camp Tecumseh with your old buddy Martin," he reminded me.

Martin — his scowling face floated between me and the rows of corn stretching away to the horizon. Whenever I dropped a ball, fumbled, or struck out, Martin was there, sneering and jeering. He stole my lunch money, copied my homework, beat me up, called me names like Drew Pee-you and Death Breath.

I sighed and leaned back in my seat. No Martin for two whole months. Maybe Dad was right. Any place would be paradise compared to Camp Tecumseh — even the House of Usher.

When Dad slowed to turn off the road, a gust of wind nudged the car. Behind us, the sky was darkening fast. It looked like the storm we'd left in Chicago had followed us all the way to Missouri.

The driveway was a narrow green tunnel burrowing uphill through trees and shaggy bushes. Shifting to first gear, Dad steered around ruts and potholes, missing some, hitting others. Branches scraped the roof and slapped the windows. While he muttered about the car's suspension system, Mom and I bounced around like Mexican jumping beans.

When Dad pulled up in front of the house, the three of us sat still for a moment and stared at the gloomy pile of bricks my great-aunt called home. Up close, it looked even worse than it had from a distance. Ivy clung to the walls, spreading over windows and doors. A wisteria vine heavy with bunches of purple blossoms twisted around the porch columns. Paint peeled, loose shutters banged in the wind, slates from the roof littered the overgrown lawn.

Charles Addams would have loved it. So would Edgar Allan Poe. But not me. No, sir, definitely not me. Just looking at the place made my skin prickle.

Dad was the first to speak. "This is your ancestral home,

2

Drew," he said, once more doing his best to sound excited. "It was built by your great-great-grandfather way back in 1865, right after the Civil War. Tylers have lived here ever since."

While Dad babbled about family history and finding your roots and things like that, I let my thoughts drift to Camp Tecumseh again. Maybe Martin wasn't so bad after all, maybe he and I could have come to terms this summer, maybe we —

My fantasies were interrupted by Great-aunt Blythe. Flinging the front door open, she came bounding down the steps. The wind ballooned her T-shirt and swirled her gray hair. If she spread her arms, she might fly up into the sky like Mary Poppins.

"Aunt Blythe, Aunt Blythe!" I was so glad to see her, I forgot the house, forgot my fears, forgot Martin. Jumping out of the car, I ran to meet her.

"Welcome to Missouri, Drew!" My aunt gave me a quick, hard hug. While I was still getting my breath, she held me at arms' length and looked me over.

"Twelve already," she said, "and shooting up faster than the weeds in my backyard. I swear you've grown two inches since I saw you at Christmas. At this rate, you'll be taller than I am in no time."

Since Aunt Blythe was barely five foot two, she wasn't exaggerating. We were almost eye to eye already.

"Don't I get a hug too?" Dad grabbed his aunt around the waist and lifted her clear off the ground.

"Put me down, you big idiot."

"Not till you tell me I'm still your favorite nephew," Dad said.

"Oh, Ward, you'll always be my favorite nephew." Aunt

Blythe winked at me. "And Drew will always be my favorite *great*-nephew."

As my aunt turned to hug Mom, Binky ran toward us, barking and leaping, leaving muddy pawprints on Dad's tan slacks. He was a little honey-colored cocker spaniel, floppy-eared and not too bright, but he and my great-aunt were inseparable. Whenever she visited us, Binky came too. He was one of the family, a sort of dim-witted second cousin, lovable in spite of his deficiencies.

When the dog calmed down, Aunt Blythe waved her arm at the house. "Well, what do you think of the old place?"

Dad shook his head. "Most people move to a condo in Florida when they're your age. They sit back, enjoy the sunshine, and forget their cares."

"*My age?*" Aunt Blythe was obviously insulted. "I'm only sixty-two, Ward. I'd be bored to death in a retirement home. I need things to do, projects to work on, challenges."

Dad put his hand up in mock surrender and backed away laughing. "You're in the right place then. I've never seen anything more challenging than this."

Aunt Blythe laughed with him. "It's a wreck," she admitted. "The roof leaks, the window frames are rotting, the front porch is in danger of collapsing — I've got my work cut out for me. If Father hadn't neglected everything, if he hadn't been so stubborn, if he'd . . ." Her voice trailed off and she shoved her hands in the pockets of her jeans.

"How is Grandfather?" Dad asked, suddenly serious.

Aunt Blythe's shoulders sagged, and for a moment, she looked tired, depressed even. "Oh, Ward, he's more cantankerous than ever."

Dad put his hand on her shoulder and gave it a little squeeze. "I hope he realizes how lucky he is to have you.

Not many daughters would come back home to take care of an old codger like him."

Aunt Blythe shrugged. "Father doesn't even know me half the time. Mother, Grandmother, Aunt Mildred — I'm somebody different every day. The past is more real to him than the present."

As she spoke, a spiral of dust and dead leaves danced up the driveway toward us like a miniature cyclone. Black clouds darkened the fields of corn across the highway. Lightning forked, and thunder rumbled. The storm had definitely caught up with us.

Aunt Blythe gave me a gentle push toward the car. "You'd better get your things before the rain starts, Drew."

Without waiting for me, my parents followed my aunt across the lawn and through the front door. By the time I'd pulled my belongings out of the back, I was all alone. Even Binky was gone.

I shouldered my daypack and turned toward the house. High up under the roof, I glimpsed a flash of white at a window. As small and pale as a face, it vanished before I had a good look at it.

Thunder boomed overhead, and a bolt of lightning zigzagged into the woods behind me, but, instead of running for shelter, I stared at the house, too scared to move. What had I seen? The little window was dark, nothing moved behind the glass, but, silly as it sounds, I couldn't get rid of the feeling that someone was watching me.

While I stood there shivering, the wind increased. It tugged at my daypack and almost yanked the duffel bag out of my hands. Thunder crashed louder than before, and lightning forked across the roof, leaping from chimney to chimney like a special effect in a Frankenstein movie. The

5

sky was an alarming purple black. Raindrops as cold and hard as marbles pelted my head and back, soaking my shirt in seconds.

More afraid of the storm than the watcher in the attic, I ran across the lawn. With every step, I told myself there were no ghosts in Aunt Blythe's house. I'd seen the reflection of a bird or a cloud in the window glass. My imagination had turned it into a face. Nobody watched, nobody waited — except my great-grandfather. It was he who expected me. Nobody else.

Chapter 2

The entrance hall was even gloomier than I'd expected. Smelling of wood smoke and the ashes of long-dead fires, it was damp and dark. Light filtered through a stained-glass window halfway up the stairs — art deco, I guess, the kind of design my mother admired in old houses in Chicago. Except for the murmur of wind and rain, the only sound was the mournful ticktock of a grandfather's clock.

Where had my aunt taken my parents? I walked to the bottom of the steps and peered up into the shadows. Not a sound from the floor above. Ahead was a long corridor. On either side, doorways opened into empty rooms. Like me, the house held its breath and listened.

Just as I was about to call out, I heard Dad's voice. "Drew's a good kid," he was saying, "but he's so insecure — worries, chews his nails, has trouble sleeping. Make sure he gets outside, exercises. Don't let him spend the whole summer with his nose in a book."

Aunt Blythe murmured something, and Dad spoke more softly. I caught a phrase here, a word there: "He's nervous . . . fearful . . . too much imagination. . . ."

Mom added her whispered opinions to Dad's. "Scared of

the dark . . . witch under the bed . . . monster in the closet. . . ."

To stop them from saying more, I dropped my daypack with a loud thud. "Where is everybody?" I yelled.

"Back here, Drew," Dad called. "In the kitchen."

Without looking at my parents, I sat down at the table and took the glass of lemonade Aunt Blythe handed me. Too angry to speak, I stuffed my mouth with sugar cookies. How could they talk about me like that? Tell my aunt I was fearful, nervous, insecure — what would she think of me?

Unaware I'd overheard his remarks, Dad began talking about his grant. Thanks to the university where he taught, he and Mom were spending the summer in southern France excavating a Roman ruin. His precious dig — once he got started there was no stopping him. He went on and on, describing fragments of this and scraps of that, things so old nobody knew what they were anymore.

To hide my feelings, I lowered my head and studied the table's scarred surface. Someone had carved a big, lopsided A into the wood. I ran my finger around its outline — up, down, across; up, down, across.

Aunt Blythe leaned toward me to see my discovery. "A for Andrew," she said, "like you."

Without answering, I kept my finger on the A. Up, down, across; up, down, across. I was cutting it deeper into the wood with each stroke. *Andrew, Andrew, Andrew* — my name, *Drew* for short.

"Starting with Captain Andrew Joseph Tyler, we've had quite a few Andrews in this family," Aunt Blythe went on.

"You're his namesake, Drew," Dad said.

Aunt Blythe smiled at my parents. "Remember the fuss Father made when he found out you'd decided not to name Drew after him?"

Mom laughed. "The way he carried on, you'd think we'd picked the most hideous name in the world for our poor baby."

Imitating the old man, Dad struck the table with his fist and scowled. "I'll not have a descendant of mine called Andrew!"

"That's why we nicknamed you *Drew*," Mom added. "We wanted to call you *Andrew,* but we shortened it to mollify your great-grandfather."

I looked up from the *A*. "Did it work?"

Dad shrugged. "We never saw him after your christening. He came back here in a snit. Never even sent you a birthday card."

While the others reminisced about Great-grandfather's legendary temper, I studied the *A*. Catching Aunt Blythe's eye, I asked her if she knew which Andrew had carved it.

"Certainly not the captain," she said. "It looks like something a boy might do when he was bored."

A loud clap of thunder made us all jump. Under the table, Binky whined.

"Poor old dog," Aunt Blythe said, "he's terrified of storms."

Dad went to the window and peered out. Turning to Mom, he said, "It looks like it's letting up. Maybe we should leave for St. Louis while we have a chance. We don't want to miss our plane."

Turning to me, he hugged me so hard I thought my ribs would crack. "Have a good summer, Drew. Behave yourself, take care of your aunt, write to us. We'll see you in eight weeks."

I clung to Dad, pressing my face against his shirt, breathing in the smell of him. Terrible scenarios raced through my head. Plane crashes, terrorists, bombs, automobile accidents. The world was full of war and danger. Nobody was safe.

"Don't go," I begged. "Please don't. What if something happens to you and Mom?"

Dad's arms tightened around me, his breath stirred my hair. "We've talked about this so many times," he said softly. "We were lucky to get the grant, Drew. Very lucky. I can't back out of the trip now."

"But there's history right here. You said so yourself. Why do you have to go all the way to France? You could set up a dig in the backyard. I'd help, I bet we'd find all kinds of old things — medicine bottles, broken china, stuff our ancestors owned."

I talked faster and faster, hoping to keep Dad from interrupting, from saying no, from leaving, but of course it didn't work.

Resting his hands on my shoulders, Dad put some space between us. "Chin up, Drew," he said firmly. "No tears. You're a big boy now."

I turned to Mom. Like Dad, she held me close, kissed me, told me she loved me. Tears shone in her eyes as she pulled away from me, but she didn't relent.

Behind me, I heard Aunt Blythe at the sink, washing dishes and pretending not to listen. If I cried, she'd know the truth — I *was* nervous, fearful, whatever else my parents had said.

"Okay, go then," I shouted. "Leave right now. See if I care!"

Mom reached out for me, but I dodged away. "I don't need you, I don't need Dad either!"

To keep from crying in front of everyone, I ran down the hall, opened the first door I saw, and dashed inside. Too late I realized the room was already occupied. An old man in a wheelchair sat beside a window. Of all the places I might have gone, I'd chosen Great-grandfather's sanctuary.

"Who is it? Who's there?" He peered at me fearfully. In the gray light, his face was skull-like, the skin stretched thin as paper over his bones, his eyes sunken.

Just as startled as he was, I stared at him. Never had I seen anyone so ancient. I wanted to run back to the kitchen, but Great-grandfather was speaking to me, one trembling hand raised as if to defend himself.

"You've come back," he quavered. "But it won't do any good. It's my house now, not yours."

Dad came into the room behind me and grabbed my arm. "What are you doing in here?" he whispered. Then, turning to the old man, he said, "Hello, Grandfather, it's Ward — remember me?"

When Great-grandfather said nothing, Dad added, "I'm Ed's son. Your grandson."

Great-grandfather made an inarticulate noise and shook his head. "Edward's dead," he muttered. "Died years ago. In a war."

"I know," Dad said, "I know. I miss him too."

Taking Great-grandfather's hand, he studied the old man's face for a moment. "This is my son, Drew, your great-grandson," he said softly. "I'm sorry he startled you, but you know how boys are — a little thoughtless sometimes, a little —"

Great-grandfather yanked his hand away from Dad. Scowling at me, he banged the floor with a cane. "Don't let him near me. I know all about him!"

Aunt Blythe rushed to his side. "What's wrong, Father? Drew didn't mean —"

Great-grandfather turned furiously to his daughter. "He's a wicked boy! Send him back where he came from, I won't have him here!"

Aunt Blythe gestured to Dad, and he led me out of the room. As soon as the door closed behind us, he said, "What on earth prompted you to bother Grandfather?"

"I just wanted to get away from you," I mumbled. "I didn't know he was in there." I tried to keep my voice from shaking but it quavered anyway. Great-grandfather had frightened me half to death.

"From the look on his face, you scared the wits out of him," Dad said. "I wonder who the devil he thought you were."

I shuddered. "Someone he didn't like very much, that's for sure."

Aunt Blythe stepped into the hall and gave me a sympathetic hug. "Lord knows who Father mistook you for," she said. "He drifts back and forth through the years as if time doesn't exist for him — at least not as we understand it."

She looked sad and tired, older too, worn down by worry. Contrite, I leaned against her side. "I'm sorry I upset him."

"Don't worry." Aunt Blythe patted my hand to show me she understood. "Father's probably forgotten about it already."

Mom was waiting for us on the porch. The worst of the storm had passed, but the rain still fell steadily. It gurgled in the downspouts and flowed over the edges of the gutter, creating a curtain of falling water. The wisteria's purple petals speckled the floor like confetti and clung to an old wooden swing. On the walls, ivy rustled as if the house were telling itself secrets.

My parents hugged and kissed me again, but they made it clear they were really leaving this time. Tears wouldn't keep them. Neither would arguments. Trying to be brave, I stood on the porch and watched the car splash downhill through the puddles in the driveway.

Aunt Blythe touched my shoulder gently. "Let's go inside, Drew. I'll take you to your room. While I fix dinner, you can unpack and make yourself at home."

Reluctantly, I followed my aunt into the shadowy hall. Now that Mom and Dad were gone, the house seemed bigger, darker, scarier. The wind and rain made sad, searching sounds. Branches tapped the windows like homeless souls begging to come in from the cold.

Overhead the floor creaked as if someone were tiptoeing from room to empty room. Startled by the noise, I glanced at my aunt, but she was striding up the steps ahead of me, talking cheerfully about the things we'd do when the rain stopped. If she sensed the presence of unseen beings, she gave no sign of it.

Down the hall behind a closed door, Great-grandfather coughed. Thinking he might emerge from his lair, I raced upstairs after Aunt Blythe. Nothing, not even a ghost, could frighten me more than that old man.

Chapter 3

Aunt Blythe led me to a small room at the top of the steps. Before she went downstairs, she gave me a hug. "I'm so glad you're here, Drew. As you can guess, Father's not much company. Most of the time, Binky and I rattle around the old place like two marbles in an empty coffee can."

Alone in the room, I did nothing for a few minutes but stand at the window. Rain poured down the glass like tears, blurring the fields and woods into a sea of ripply green. Near the house, trees tossed and swayed. At the bottom of the hill, the highway stretched northward, leading to Illinois and Iowa, and southward to St. Louis. It was a lonely view, just right for a lonely person.

"Make yourself at home," Aunt Blythe had said, but I didn't think that was possible. Home to me was a modern apartment in Chicago, furnished with sleek Scandinavian imports. The only old things were Dad's artifacts displayed in brightly lit glass cases.

In my aunt's house, I was surrounded by antiques. A tall, carved headboard leaned ominously over the bed I was supposed to sleep in. A spooky wardrobe with mirrored doors lurked in a corner. Bureau, rocking chair, desk, bookcase — everything in the room had been owned by other people. Dead people. The thought made me shiver.

To chase the ghosts away, I turned on the lamp, but its light made the shadows bigger and darker. I was tempted to run down to the kitchen, but the memory of Dad's words stopped me. "Fearful, nervous, insecure" — wasn't that what he'd told Aunt Blythe? She'd already seen me behave like a baby once today. I didn't want to give a repeat performance.

I'd unpack, I'd put my things away, I'd try to make myself at home.

For the next twenty or thirty minutes, I kept myself busy. I filled the bureau with a jumble of socks, underwear, T-shirts, and jeans. I made room in the bookcase for the paperbacks I'd brought with me. I found a place on the desk for a picture of Mom and Dad and me. I taped posters to the walls — a surfer riding a huge wave, the Chicago skyline, a sailboat on Lake Michigan, the stone lions in front of the Art Institute.

Left with a pair of shoes and a windbreaker, I opened the door opposite my bed. Instead of finding a closet, I was surprised to see a flight of steps. Almost blocked by piles of magazines and boxes of old clothes, they led up to a dark attic.

Cold, damp air blew down into my face, tickling my nose with the smell of dust. At the same moment, the floor creaked right over my head.

The first thing I thought of was the flash of white I'd seen at the attic window. Was someone hiding up there? Had it been his footsteps I'd heard earlier? His eyes I'd felt? Slamming the door shut, I pressed my ear against the wood and listened. Except for the pounding of my own heart, I heard nothing. The attic was silent.

Backing away from the door, I let my breath out in a long sigh. No one was hiding in the attic. Or anywhere else. In old houses, floors creaked all the time. Why did I always let my imagination run wild? It seemed to me I'd been born with eyes and ears that saw and heard things nobody else noticed — monsters in the shadows, footsteps in the dark.

Downstairs, the hall clock struck six. Maybe it was dinnertime. Surely I smelled roast chicken. Taking the steps two at a time, I followed my nose straight to the kitchen.

Aunt Blythe was standing at the stove, her back to me. When I entered the room, she turned around, a spoon in her hand, and smiled. "I hope you like spaghetti, Drew."

I stared at the bubbling tomato sauce. "Where's the chicken?"

Aunt Blythe looked at me. "Chicken?"

Steam rose from boiling water and misted the kitchen windows. The scent of oregano filled my nose.

"When I was upstairs, I smelled roast chicken," I said. "I know I did."

"Your nose was playing tricks on you, Drew." Aunt Blythe smiled and picked up a box. Dumping long straws of pasta into the pot, she said, "I'll fix chicken tomorrow night."

Great-grandfather joined us for dinner. Before he appeared, I heard the squeak of his wheelchair in the hall. I glanced at my aunt, but she just smiled.

"Brace yourself," she said. "We'll probably have to introduce you all over again."

Great-grandfather wheeled himself into position at the head of the dining room table. Aunt Blythe fastened a large plastic bib around his neck, the kind you sometimes get in a seafood restaurant. When she was finished, he fingered his silverware. His hands were bent and twisted, the backs roped with blue veins, the skin discolored.

Finally, he raised his head and looked at me. "Andrew," he mumbled. "Andrew."

Aunt Blythe smiled, obviously pleased that he'd remembered my name. "That's right, Father. Isn't it nice to have him here?"

Great-grandfather scowled. "No," he muttered, "not nice at all. Told you I don't want him in the house. Hasn't changed a bit, just as bad as ever, can't fool me."

He shot me a look of such pure hatred that I froze, fork halfway to my mouth, and stared at him. Backing away from the table like an angry child, he turned his wheelchair and propelled himself toward his room.

Aunt Blythe scurried after him. "Father," she said, "for heaven's sake, come eat your dinner!"

I sat at the table alone, staring at my spaghetti. Outside, the rain fell steadily. The wind blew and the house creaked like an old sailing ship caught in a storm far from port.

When Aunt Blythe returned, she apologized. "I don't understand why Father's so hateful to you. He won't listen to a word I say."

I watched her put Great-grandfather's dinner on a tray. "I think it might be best to let him eat in his room tonight. Go ahead, Drew. I'll join you as soon as I can."

The minutes crept by, marked by the slow ticktock, ticktock of the hall clock. Bushes tapped on the windows, an icy draft eddied around my ankles, the house continued to murmur and groan. Under the table, Binky shivered and crept close to me. Laying his head on my feet, he whimpered.

By the time my aunt returned, her spaghetti sauce had

congealed in a cold puddle. She apologized again and ate quickly.

After dinner, Aunt Blythe lit a fire to drive off the storm's chill. While I read a paperback I'd brought from home, she worked on a patchwork quilt. Binky snoozed on a cushion by the hearth. In his room, behind a closed door, Great-grandfather slept.

Looking up from my book, I watched Aunt Blythe's needle flash in and out. Almost finished, the quilt spread across her lap and fell to the floor in a heap of bright calico.

When my aunt noticed I was studying the design, she told me the pattern was called Tumbling Blocks. "It's an optical illusion, Drew. You can't tell the tops of the blocks from the bottoms. When you look at them, they seem to shift back and forth."

I stared at the quilt. Aunt Blythe was right. The pattern changed directions, teased my eyes. "It's like the one on my bed," I said. "Only mine's older."

Aunt Blythe nodded. "Great-aunt Mildred made that quilt almost a hundred years ago."

The fire hissed and popped and sent a shower of sparks flying up the chimney. I leaned closer to my aunt. "Do you ever wonder about the people who used to live in this house?"

"What do you mean, Drew?"

"Well, so many of their belongings are still here — things they touched, things they made. It just seems strange. . . ." While I spoke, I looked around the room, finding faded photographs on the mantel, a pair of china dolls sharing a child-sized rocking chair, shelves of old books. My voice trailed off. I wasn't sure what I was trying to say.

Aunt Blythe ran one finger over the row of stitches she'd just finished. "Things last longer than people," she said softly.

That was true, but it wasn't what I meant. "The people, our ancestors — do you think they're still here somehow?"

"Are we talking about ghosts?"

"Do you believe in them?"

Unlike some adults, Aunt Blythe took my question seriously. Leaning her head back, she stared into the fire and thought about her answer. "In an old house, the past is all around you," she said slowly. "You hear sounds sometimes, even smell things."

"Like roast chicken?"

She nodded. "Superstitious people might call it the work of ghosts, but I think of them as echoes, little traces of the folks who once called this house home. Nothing to be scared of."

A gust of wind spattered raindrops against the window. Binky twitched and whimpered in his sleep. Suddenly raising his head, he stared at the doorway as if he saw something in the dark hall.

At the same moment, the clock whirred and began to chime. Startled by the sound, I jumped.

"Goodness," Aunt Blythe said, "why are we talking about things like this at bedtime? Don't listen to me, Drew. I'm just being fanciful. I've never seen a ghost in this house. Or anywhere else for that matter."

Shaking her head at her own silliness, my aunt shifted the quilt and began to outline the next block with small, neat stitches. "Run along, Drew. I'll be up in a few minutes."

At the foot of the steps, I hesitated. The second floor was dark. Above it and even darker was the attic. While I hesitated, a draft fluttered the curtains at the window on the landing. They moved as silently as ghosts, I thought, pale and filmy, almost transparent.

Aunt Blythe pressed a switch and flooded the stairs with light. Giving me a little swat on the rear end, she said, "Sleep tight, Drew."

I used the bathroom as quickly as I could and raced down the hall past one, two, three closed doors. Pulling my quilt over my head, I curled up with a flashlight and read until I heard Aunt Blythe coming up the steps.

Hours later, something woke me — a faint sound above my head. The attic door opened a crack, and cold air swirled through the room. The house moved and creaked and groaned like an old person stirring in his sleep.

Almost too scared to breathe, I watched the door. Minutes passed. When I was sure nothing was hiding behind it, I eased out of bed, closed the door, and shoved the rocking chair in front of it.

Still frightened, I tiptoed into the hall and leaned over the bannister. "Binky," I whispered, "Binky, come here."

In a few seconds, the dog trotted up the steps, grinning lopsidedly at me.

"Good boy." Holding him tight, I got into bed and patted the quilt beside me. "Stay," I begged, "stay."

Binky licked my nose, wagged his tail, turned around a couple of times, and made himself comfortable. Hoping I was safe, I closed my eyes and willed myself to sleep.

Chapter 4

The next morning, it was still raining, the gray, steady kind that can last for days, maybe even weeks. To give us something to do, Aunt Blythe offered to take me on a tour of the house. Since I'd already seen most of it, the first floor didn't take long — living room, dining room, sewing room, kitchen, pantry, and Great-grandfather's bedroom.

Tiptoeing past his closed door, Aunt Blythe said, "No sense disturbing Father. He woke early, I gave him breakfast, now he's napping."

Upstairs, there were five bedrooms — mine, Aunt Blythe's, and three others, all empty. Dust lay thick on the bare floors, and cobwebs filmed the windows. The furniture was gone, sold long ago to an antique dealer in St. Louis.

When Aunt Blythe saw the rocker in front of the attic door, I said, "The wind kept rattling it. I couldn't sleep, so I . . ." Too embarrassed to continue, I shoved the rocker back to its corner.

Aunt Blythe opened the door. "Goodness, I haven't been in the attic for years." Shoving a pile of *National Geographics* out of her way, she scrambled up the steps.

At the top, she paused and looked down at me. "Come

on, Drew. Junk, trash, treasure — you name it, it's here."

I hesitated. Even in the daytime the attic was spooky. I didn't like its musty smell or the sound of the wind and rain on the roof. Spiders, mice — who knew what was hiding up there?

Binky whimpered to get my attention, then backed away and wagged his tail. His big brown eyes seemed to say, "Don't go. You'll be sorry if you do."

"Silly old dog," Aunt Blythe said. "For some reason, the attic spooks him. Whenever I open the door, he runs in the opposite direction."

Ashamed to admit I was every bit as scared as Binky, I forced myself to climb the stairs. The attic was cold and damp, as silent as an undisturbed tomb and just as unwelcoming. Furniture draped in sheets rose up like ghosts. A glimpse of my reflection in a huge gilt mirror startled me. A headless dressmaker's dummy lurked in the shadows. It was hard to move without stumbling over something — boxes, stacks of books and records, moldy heaps of magazines and newspapers, broken appliances, ice skates, shoes, toys.

"Be careful," Aunt Blythe said. "The floor's riddled with dry rot."

Forgetting her own warning, she plunged ahead, opening trunks and boxes, poking and pawing through things, reminiscing. She'd worn this dress to her first dance, she'd knitted that scarf. The sled in the corner had belonged to her brother, the bicycle beside it was hers. There was her dollhouse. Here was her high-school diploma.

Cobwebs stuck to my face, spiders scurried across my feet. In the walls, something rustled. The wind made a moaning sound and I shivered. "It's cold up here."

Aunt Blythe was too busy rummaging through the contents of an old trunk to listen to me. "I've been looking for these." She held up a handful of old photographs. "I can't imagine what they're doing here. They belong in the family album."

Curious in spite of myself, I watched my aunt fan the pictures out like a pack of playing cards. Studying the old-fashioned, fading faces, I picked one to ask about. "Who is she?"

Aunt Blythe stared at the picture. Head tilted to one side, a girl smiled into the camera lens. She wore a lace-trimmed dress and her dark hair was piled loosely on top of her head. Her eyes sparkled as if the photographer had said something funny.

"That's Hannah," Aunt Blythe said, "my first cousin once removed."

Pleased to have such a beautiful relative, I watched my aunt touch the girl's face lovingly. "I adored her when I was a child, Drew, but she and Father never got along. Every time they saw each other, they quarreled about something. Politics usually."

"Is she still alive?"

Aunt Blythe thought a moment. "I really don't know," she said slowly. "Goodness, Hannah would be well over ninety by now, but she had ten times the energy of the average person. It's hard to imagine her slowing down long enough to die."

Bending her head over the photograph, she smiled at Hannah. "I wouldn't be a bit surprised to hear she's still alive and just as feisty as ever."

Shuffling the pictures, Aunt Blythe found another one of Hannah sitting in a porch swing beside a younger boy. A man and woman stood behind them. All four looked solemn.

"Theo," Aunt Blythe said. "According to Father, he was a no-good rascal, but just look at that angelic little face. He couldn't have been all bad."

"I guess Great-grandfather didn't like him either."

"No, indeed." Aunt Blythe laughed. "If anything, Father disliked Theo even more than Hannah. The feeling was mutual, I'm afraid. I haven't seen either one of them since their mother died. Lord, that was more than fifty years ago."

I looked closely at the swing in the picture. "Was this taken on your porch?"

Aunt Blythe nodded. "Hannah used to live here. Father bought the house after her mother died." She pointed to the sweet-faced woman and the stern man beside her. "Great-aunt Mildred and Great-uncle Henry."

I leaned against my aunt's shoulder. "Let me guess," I said. "Great-grandfather didn't like them either."

"What a perceptive boy you are." Aunt Blythe sighed. "Poor Father. Sometimes I think he hates the whole world, including himself."

We looked at the rest of the pictures. Hannah and Theo grew older, and so did their parents. The last one had been taken on Hannah's wedding day.

Aunt Blythe tapped the groom's face. "John Larkin," she said. "If I'd met a man like him, I might have gotten married myself."

Laughing at her foolishness, she stacked the photographs in a neat pile. "I have half a mind to put these back in the album where they belong," she said. "Father must have taken them out and stashed them up here. He doesn't like to be reminded this was once his uncle's house."

While Aunt Blythe was talking, I noticed a photograph

lying on the floor. I bent to pick it up and found I was staring at a faded likeness of my own face — my eyes, my nose, my mouth, my hair, even my glum expression. Only the boy's clothes were different. He wore a white shirt with a stiff collar, a tie, knee-length trousers, dark stockings, and ankle-high lace-up shoes, brand new from the stiff, shiny look of them. With his hands in his pockets, my twin stared at me across the years that separated us. My double, my other self. Looking at him gave me goose bumps.

I thrust the picture at my aunt. "Who's this?" I whispered. "Do you know?"

Aunt Blythe drew in her breath. "My goodness, Drew, he looks exactly like you." Turning the photograph over, she examined the back. No name, no date, only the address of a photographer in St. Louis and the assurance that the negative was on file and more prints could be ordered.

Staring at my double, she said slowly, "I think Hannah had two brothers. Yes, I'm sure she did. Theo and, and — this boy."

I shook my head. "If he's Hannah's brother, why isn't he in any of the other pictures?"

Aunt Blythe didn't answer right away. In the silence, rain pattered against the windows and dripped through holes in the roof. The wind crept in through cracks and stirred the folds of a long white dress hanging from the rafters.

Finally, my aunt raised her eyes from the photograph. "I think his name was Andrew. Isn't that strange? You share a face and a name with a boy who died years before you were born."

My throat tightened. "He died? Andrew died?"

Aunt Blythe looked at me. "Oh, dear," she said, "I didn't mean to frighten you."

"I'm not scared!" My voice came out as high and squeaky as a girl's. Furious at myself for being such a baby, I leapt to my feet and headed for the stairs.

"Slow down, Drew," my aunt called. "You'll go through the floor!"

Before the words were out of her mouth, a board split under my weight, and I fell flat on my face.

In seconds my aunt was beside me. "Are you all right?" she asked. "Did you hurt yourself?"

"I'm fine." Too embarrassed to meet her eyes, I peered into the hole I'd made. Something was hidden in the dark space under the floor. Forgetting Andrew, I lifted out an old wooden cigar box grimy with layers of dust and cobwebs.

Maybe I'd found a treasure. Setting the box down, I slowly raised the lid. Inside was a candle, a piece of chalk, a few wooden matches, and a bulging leather bag that clinked when I shook it.

I looked at my aunt. "What do you think is inside? Gold coins? Jewels?"

"I can't guess," she admitted. "Open it, Drew."

Holding my breath, I untied the knot and tipped the pouch. A stream of marbles poured out, nudging and bumping one another, overflowing my hands, spinning across the floor in all directions.

I watched them roll away, too disappointed to care where they went, but Aunt Blythe went after them on her hands and knees. Pressing one into my hand, she said, "This is a genuine aggie, Drew, a perfect bull's-eye, the finest I've ever seen."

The marble was about an inch in diameter, ruby red with a swirl at the top like the white of an eye. Smooth and warm, it had a lucky feel.

Gathering the others, Aunt Blythe named them: immies, moonstones, carnelians, cat's-eyes, rainbows, peppermint stripes. Some were made of glass, some of semiprecious stones, some of clay. They were old, she said, in good condition and probably very valuable.

"How do you know so much about marbles?" I asked.

"You may not believe this, but I was the playground champion in grade school. I won so many marbles, they filled three coffee cans. By sixth grade, the boys refused to play with me. They said it was because I was a girl, but I knew the real reason — they couldn't beat me."

Sitting back on her heels, Aunt Blythe studied the marbles silently. After a while, she said, "These meant a lot to somebody once. I wonder who hid them here — and why."

I'd already found the answer. At the bottom of the pouch was a piece of folded paper. The ink was faded, the handwriting old-fashioned and full of curlicues, but the message was clear:

WARNING

These marbles belong to

ANDREW JOSEPH TYLER

If you take them you will be sorry.

7 June 1910

At the bottom, Andrew had drawn a fierce skull and crossbones.

After she'd read the message, Aunt Blythe picked up the picture of my double and studied it. "The poor child must have hidden them up here before he died."

Without looking at my aunt, I dropped Andrew's aggie into the pouch, then the immies, the moonstones, the cat's-eyes — click, click, clickety click. The sound was loud in the silent attic.

"What are you doing, Drew?"

"We have to put everything back the way we found it."

"Don't be silly. We can't leave those marbles in that dirty hole. A collector would pay a small fortune for them."

I glanced at the piece of paper lying on the floor near her shoe. "You saw the note."

Despite my protests, Aunt Blythe dropped the pouch into her pocket. "Please try to understand. The house needs a new roof, new wiring, new plumbing. A good painting. Andrew lived here once, this was his home, I'm sure he'd approve."

"No," I cried, surprising myself with the strength of my feelings. "No, you mustn't take them. They belong here, Aunt Blythe."

She refused to listen. At the top of the steps, she turned to me and said, "If Andrew comes looking for his marbles, I promise to take full responsibility for him."

Her words made me shiver. It was wrong to joke about the dead, wrong to steal from them. Dropping the cigar box into the hole, I fled downstairs behind my aunt.

Chapter 5

Before I went to bed that night, Aunt Blythe said, "I've been thinking about the marbles, Drew. If you're really worried, I'll put them back. Would that make you feel better?"

I was standing at the foot of the steps, afraid to go to my room, but ashamed to admit it. Without looking at my aunt, I picked at a fleck of peeling paint on the bannister. "Can we do it now?"

"Not in the dark." Aunt Blythe shuddered. "We'd probably fall through the floor."

"First thing in the morning then."

"Right after breakfast." She seized my hand and gave it a firm shake, a promise. "Go to bed now. It's past ten."

Slowly, I climbed to the landing. Above me the hall was dark. I'd forgotten to turn on the light at the bottom of the steps. If I went back, I'd prove I was a baby, scared of everything.

I put my foot on the first step and gripped the bannister. All I had to do was run up the rest of the steps, dash through my door, flick a switch, and leap into bed. I'd be safe in my own room. But I couldn't lift my other foot. It was like jumping off the high dive — the more you thought about it, the worse it seemed.

Suddenly, my scalp tightened. Something moved in the shadows above me. For a second, I saw a flickering image as insubstantial as a drawing on air. Two women stood outside my door. They wore long dresses and clung to each other, sobbing, their faces hidden.

Before I could make a sound, they vanished. The hall was empty. Moonlight patterned the walls and floor with shifting shadows. What had I seen? I didn't know, couldn't be sure. The figures had disappeared too quickly.

Beside me, the window curtains stirred in a breeze. It was cold on the landing. I wanted to fling myself into my aunt's arms and beg her to protect me, I wanted to jump into bed and pull the quilt over my head, but I was too scared to move. The ghosts might appear again, they might be waiting for me, they could be hiding anywhere.

Upstairs, the hall floor creaked, and Binky appeared at the top of the steps, grinning down at me. I took a deep breath and ran to him, scooped him up, hugged his warm, furry body. He'd protect me, keep me safe.

"Are they gone?" I whispered.

"Whuff." Binky licked my cheek and wagged his tail.

Holding the dog tightly, I looked around. The hall was definitely empty. I carried him into my room and turned on the light. Everything was the way I'd left it. No sobbing ladies in long dresses. No Andrew either.

Once more, I shoved the rocking chair in front of the attic door. Undressing quickly, I got into bed and put my arms around Binky. "You didn't see them, did you? If they'd been here, you would've barked."

Binky wagged his tail again, and I relaxed a tiny bit. "It was just my imagination, wasn't it?"

"Whuff."

Hoping *whuff* meant yes, I pulled the dog under the quilt with me and tried to fall asleep.

The next thing I knew, I was dreaming about a rocket ship traveling through space at hyperspeed. The captain had his back to me. He wore a jacket quilted with tumbling blocks. I couldn't see his face, but I knew he was old. Very old.

Suddenly a shower of marbles spun toward us out of the blackness — moonstones, cat's-eyes, immies, blood-red aggies. Like meteorites, they trailed fire. They struck the window, clickety click. They bounced and knocked against the ship's sides, clickety clickety click.

"You found them," the old man said. "Don't deny it. If he comes for them, you must take full responsibility."

When the captain turned and looked at me, it was my own face I saw. "Andrew," I cried. "Andrew!"

Wide awake, I sat up in bed and stared at the ceiling. Overhead, things bumped and clattered. Someone was in the attic. Then I heard his footsteps coming down the stairs slowly, one step at a time. I knew who it was, I knew what he wanted.

Binky knew too. He looked at the attic door and whimpered. Before I could stop him, he leapt off the bed and ran. I wanted to go after him, I wanted to call Aunt Blythe, but it was too late. The door was opening, pushing the rocking chair ahead of it.

On the threshold, a boy appeared. Except for the white nightshirt he wore, it might have been me. For a moment, he leaned against the door frame, struggling to catch his breath. When he stepped away from the wall, he tottered and almost fell. I heard him mutter something that sounded like *drat*.

A few feet from the bed, Andrew stopped and stared at me, his eyes wide with surprise. "Who are you?" he whispered hoarsely. "What are you doing here?"

I opened my mouth, but no words came out. Clutching the quilt, I shook my head. *Let me be dreaming,* I prayed, *oh, please let me still be dreaming. Make him go away.*

Andrew came closer instead. I heard his bare feet patter across the floor. Without looking, I knew he was leaning over me, breathing hard. "Why, you're no bigger than I am," he muttered. "How dare you sneak into my house, steal my things, and then try to hide yourself in my bed?"

Before I knew what he was doing, Andrew grabbed my shoulders and tried to pull me out of bed. The effort made him cough. Letting me go, he leaned against the wall and gasped for breath. When he finally spoke, his voice was weak but still threatening. "If you don't give me my marbles at once, I shall call Papa. He's a lawyer, he'll have you locked up in jail so fast your head will spin."

I was crying now, I couldn't help it. "I'll give them to you tomorrow," I sobbed. "I promise, Andrew, I promise."

He held out his hand. It shook a little. "I want my marbles now!"

"My aunt has them — she said you had no use for marbles, she said you were dead."

Andrew drew in his breath. "I don't know who your aunt is or where she got such a fantastical notion. I'm not dead, as you can plainly see. Give me my marbles, you thief, and get out of my bed at once."

"Please go away," I begged. "This is my bed. You don't live here anymore. You, you —" For some reason, I couldn't bring myself to tell him again that he was dead, especially when he was so sure he wasn't. "I'm sorry about the marbles, honest I am. I told my aunt not to take them, but she . . ."

Stumbling over words, repeating things I'd already said, I went on talking till I realized Andrew wasn't listening. He was prowling around the room, bumping into furniture like a blind man lost in a strange place. For the first time, he seemed to sense something was wrong.

"Where is my sister?" he asked. "When I went to the attic, she was fast asleep in that chair. Surely you saw her."

We both looked at the empty rocker. "Hannah doesn't live here either," I whispered. "She's very old now, almost a hundred — Aunt Blythe said so."

Andrew leaned over the bed and stared down at me. His face was deathly pale, but the skin below his eyes was dark.

"The fever," he whispered, "it's driven me out of my head. I'm standing here looking at my own self lying in bed. You aren't real, I'm dreaming, walking in my sleep."

Seizing the quilt, Andrew tried to jerk it out of my hands, but I held tight. Once more the effort exhausted him. "There's no sense fetching Papa," he muttered. "Hannah will know what to do, she always does."

I watched him go to the door and peer into the hall. "Hannah," he called. "Where are you?"

The house was silent. No one stirred. No one replied.

When Andrew turned to me, I realized he was even more frightened than I was. "Surely Hannah wouldn't leave. She promised Mama she'd stay with me all night. I heard them crying outside my door."

My scalp prickled. The sobbing women in the hall — had they been Andrew's mother and sister? No, no, this couldn't be happening. I closed my eyes. *Let him be gone when I open them, please, please, let him be gone.*

But no matter how badly I wanted him to disappear,

Andrew stayed where he was, leaning against the door frame and gasping for air. The rasping sound of his breath made me shudder. At any moment I expected him to collapse, to die all over again before my eyes.

"You can't be alive," I whispered, "you can't — it's impossible."

"Do I look as bad as that?" Andrew came back to the bed and sat on the edge, close enough for me to see the fear in his eyes. "Dr. Fulton told Mama I was like to die before morning, but he saved me from blood poisoning last year and measles the year before that, and croup and whooping cough as well. Hannah lived through diphtheria. She says I will too."

He smiled uncertainly. "I hope Hannah is right, but the truth is I feel very weak. And cold. I should be in bed. If you don't let me under the covers, you'll surely be the death of me."

When Andrew reached for the quilt once more, I pulled it over my head. I didn't want to see his face again. I had to make him leave, I couldn't stand it anymore. "The cold can't hurt you," I cried. "Nothing can. You're already dead! Go back to your grave, rest in peace, let me be!"

Andrew yanked the covers away and forced me to look at him. "That's a wicked lie," he gasped. "If I'd died, I'd know it, I'd remember. Surely death is too powerful a thing to miss altogether."

The doubt in his voice made me braver. Switching on the lamp beside the bed, I cried, "Look, just look. Is this your room?"

Half-blinded, Andrew crouched at the foot of the bed and shielded his eyes from the brilliant electric light. When he finally lowered his hands, he gazed around the room, taking in my posters, my running shoes, my jeans draped over the rocker, the radio. "Where are my pictures, my books?" he whispered. "What have you done with my things?"

"Great-grandfather got rid of them years ago." My voice shook with the power of truth. Harsh truth. Cruel truth. I was frightening Andrew, but I had to make him see this wasn't his house anymore. No matter what he thought, he couldn't stay here.

Andrew shook his head, still unconvinced. Ignoring his tears, I pointed to the calendar hanging above the bookcase. "See what year it is?"

He got to his feet and tottered across the room for a closer look. "No," he said, "no, that can't be right. It's 1910, I'm twelve years old, I have my whole life ahead of me."

Fighting fear and pity, I watched him press his hand to his chest. Before I realized what he was doing, he was back at the bed, grabbing my hand and holding it against his left side. "Feel that?" he whispered. "I can't be dead."

Under my palm, Andrew's heart pounded rapidly against his ribs. His skin was warm, his flesh solid over his bones. On the wall beside the bed, his shadow merged with mine.

I jerked my hand away, frightened by the living feel of him. Nothing made sense. Ghosts were transparent, insubstantial, they didn't cast shadows, they didn't have beating hearts.

For a moment, neither of us spoke. We sat on the bed staring at each other.

Andrew finally said, "I don't understand. If you, if I, if we both . . ." His words trailed away in confusion. Even though the room was warm, he shivered.

My thoughts were muddled too, but I knew one thing

for sure. No matter how badly I wanted to be rid of Andrew, I'd brought him here. If I let him return to the past, he'd die. But he wouldn't be gone. Every time I passed a mirror, I'd see his face. Every time I spoke, I'd hear his voice. His ghost would haunt me forever.

Whether Andrew realized it or not, it wasn't his marbles he'd come for. It was his life.

Chapter 6

The room was so quiet I could hear Andrew's breath rattle in his chest. There was no other sound. The hall clock was silent. The curtains hung motionless at the window. Not a car, not a truck, not a plane disturbed the silence.

"How did I come here?" Andrew asked. "How do I go back?" He sat as still as stone, his eyes fixed on my face, waiting for me to explain.

"It's got something to do with the marbles," I said uncertainly. "Why did you hide them?"

He shrugged. "I wanted to put them where they'd be safe. They're mine, I won them all, mostly from my cousin. I thought he'd take them while I was sick. That's how Edward is. You can't trust him, he's always sneaking around. There's no telling what he'd do if he had the chance."

While he talked, Andrew traced the pattern on the quilt, his finger moving from one block to the next. "Mama made this for me when I was a baby," he said softly. "The colors have faded so much I scarcely recognize it, but this is her stitching. She sewed every thread."

Keeping his head down, Andrew studied the rows of tiny stitches as if he were reading a message from the past. He breathed deeply, slowly, deliberately.

37

To get his attention, I touched his hand. "Tell me everything that happened tonight."

Andrew thought hard. "I heard Mama and Hannah crying. They were in the hall, right outside my door. I wanted to say Dr. Fulton was wrong, I wasn't going to die, but I couldn't open my mouth, couldn't speak, couldn't even raise my head. Then Hannah sat down in that rocker."

He pointed to the chair I'd shoved in front of the attic door. "She said she'd watch me all night, she wouldn't leave me, she wouldn't let me die."

He rested a moment as if talking wearied him. "I guess I fell asleep. I dreamed my marbles were spinning through the air. I tried to catch them, but they flew away from me, getting smaller and smaller."

When he paused again for breath, I said, "I dreamed about marbles too. I was in a spaceship and they were coming toward me like a meteor shower — cat's-eyes, immies, moonstones, aggies. . . ."

Paying no attention to me, Andrew went on talking. "All of a sudden, I woke up. Maybe it was the dream, but I was sure someone had stolen my marbles."

He looked at the empty rocking chair. "Hannah was sleeping right there. I sneaked past her, just as quiet as a shadow, and *floated* up the attic steps. It was as if I'd turned to smoke, I had no weight at all. I saw the hole in the floor. The cigar box was there, but the marbles were gone. Then the attic turned pitch black and everything spun round and round and round. The next thing I knew, I was in this room and you were in my bed."

Andrew let out his breath in a long sigh that made him cough. When he could speak, he said, "Maybe that's what dying's like — floating away, leaving everything behind,

38

never coming back." He leaned toward me, his eyes fever bright. "Do you suppose I died, after all?"

I shook my head. "I think you woke up just in time. If you'd stayed asleep, if you hadn't gone upstairs to look for your marbles, you'd probably be dead right now."

"Are you saying I came here instead of dying?" Andrew asked. "Like the man in *The Time Machine* who went to the future?"

It was too fantastic to be true, but neither of us could come up with another explanation. As far as we could see, a hole had opened between Andrew's time and mine, and he'd fallen through.

"If I go back, I'll die," Andrew said. "But what will keep me alive here? Look at me. I'm still deathly ill."

"Modern medicine can cure just about anything."

Andrew clutched my arms. "Call a doctor," he begged. "I'll take the medicine no matter how bad it tastes. Then, when I'm well, I'll —"

I interrupted him. "But who will I say you are? How will I explain you? People don't just appear out of nowhere."

"Lord A'mighty," Andrew exclaimed. "Have you no brains? We're as alike as two peas in a pod. All we need to do is switch places. I'll get in bed. You go up to the attic and hide."

The excitement wore Andrew out. He began coughing again, harder this time. "Switch clothes with me," he begged. "Quick, or it'll be too late. I've used up almost all my strength."

I glanced uneasily at our reflections in the mirror over my dresser. Except for our clothes, we were identical. If I put on his nightshirt, would I still be me? Suppose I turned into him? Maybe *I'd* die of diphtheria instead of Andrew.

"What are you waiting for?" Andrew was struggling with his buttons, fumble-fingered, shaky with fever. "Aren't you going to help me?"

I'd gone too far to turn back. Swallowing my fear, I pulled off my pajamas and helped Andrew out of his nightshirt. He was so weak I had to poke his arms into the pajama sleeves, button the front, and guide his legs into the pants. Carefully, I eased him into bed and covered him with the quilt.

"Your name," he whispered. "I don't know your name."

"It's the same as yours, only they call me Drew for short."

"My marbles, my face, my name — you stole everything, didn't you?" Andrew lay back and closed his eyes. His breathing rasped, his chest rattled. "Well, don't steal my life too, Drew. For the Lord's sake, save me."

Frightened by the change in him, I ran across the hall and rapped on my aunt's door. "Aunt Blythe, Aunt Blythe, come quick. I don't feel well."

In a voice fuzzy with sleep, she said, "Just a minute, Drew, I'll be right there."

Back in my room, I leaned over Andrew. His eyes were still closed, and he was struggling to breathe. "Don't die," I begged him, "hang on, Andrew, she's coming, she'll get a doctor."

"Hannah," he murmured, "fetch Hannah."

Turning away from Andrew, I shouted, "Hurry, Aunt Blythe, please hurry!"

The moment her door opened, I crept up the steps to the attic and hid in the shadows. In the room below, Aunt Blythe said, "What's wrong, Drew?"

Andrew moaned.

"Heavens," Aunt Blythe cried, "you're burning with fever."

As she spoke, the air around me darkened and thickened. The floor tilted and began to spin round and round, faster and faster. To keep from falling, I reached out and grabbed at things, but they whirled away from me as if they had no substance. Which way was up? Which way down? The world was tumbling and so was I.

My ears roared, my head ached, my heart pounded, I couldn't get my breath. Dying — I was dying of diphtheria. Andrew had tricked me, he'd traded my life for his. Too dizzy to stand, I plunged into a terrible whirling blackness.

Chapter 7

When I opened my eyes, everything was still. The gray light of early morning silvered the bare floor. Far away, a train whistle blew, a sad, lonely sound.

Slowly, I got to my feet. What was I doing in the attic? Dreams and strange ideas floated through my head, but I was too confused to think straight. Bed, I ought to be in bed.

Convinced I was walking in my sleep, I tiptoed to the top of the stairs and inched my way down. When I woke up, I'd be safe in my own room. Everything would be fine.

I eased the attic door open. There was my bed waiting for me, quilt flung back, pillows askew. All I had to do was get in and pull the covers up. I'd be safe.

I took one step into the room and stopped dead. Hannah was sleeping in the rocking chair — just where Andrew said she'd be. I hadn't dreamed, hadn't walked in my sleep. Wide awake, I was wearing Andrew's nightshirt, standing in his room, staring at his sister.

Hoping to escape before the Tylers awoke, I crept back up the steps, but a quick look told me it wasn't the attic I'd explored with Aunt Blythe — there was no clutter, no broken appliances, no junk, just a few trunks and crates. I gripped a rafter tightly, closed my eyes, and concentrated all my energy on Andrew. "Please," I whispered, "please come back. Don't leave me here."

Nothing happened. Outside, birds cheeped softly. The sky was lightening, turning pink. At any moment, Hannah would open her eyes and see the empty bed. What would she think? What would she do?

Heart pounding, I sneaked down the stairs to the bedroom. Hannah was still asleep. I tiptoed past her, slid into bed, and lay motionless, scarcely daring to breathe, afraid the slightest noise would wake her.

Without turning my head, I gazed around the room, taking in as much as I could. The furniture, including the bed, was the same, but flowered paper covered the walls, a pattern of tiny blue roses repeated endlessly against a beige background. White curtains fluttered at the windows. A round picture of three horses' heads hung above the bureau.

My eyes kept returning to Andrew's sister. Hannah — not an old woman in her nineties but a girl fourteen or fifteen years old, even prettier than the faded photograph I'd seen of her. She wore a long white dress, wrinkled and creased from a night in the rocking chair. Her feet were bare. Her dark hair tumbled down around her face.

Suddenly, she moved, changed position, yawned. It was like seeing a picture come to life. When she raised her fists to rub sleep from her eyes, I shut mine.

Holding my breath, I lay as still as death and listened to Hannah walk toward the bed. She leaned over me and whispered Andrew's name, my name, touching my skin with soft, warm fingers. She was no dream, no ghost.

"Mama," she cried, "Mama, come quick!"

A door opened, and footsteps raced toward me.

"His fever's gone, Mama. He's still alive." Hannah's voice shook and she burst into tears.

"Praise be," a woman whispered. "Open your eyes, Andrew, look at me."

Dumb with fear, I stared at Mrs. Tyler. Even if I'd wanted to, I couldn't have spoken. Suppose I didn't sound like Andrew? Suppose I said the wrong thing? Surely they'd know I was an imposter.

Alarmed by my silence, Mrs. Tyler told Hannah to call Dr. Fulton. "His eyes, the way he looks at me — you'd think the boy had never seen me before."

Hannah ran downstairs, leaving me alone with Andrew's mother, a kind-faced stranger I'd glimpsed once in an old photo album. Never doubting I was her son, Mrs. Tyler stroked my hair. "Are you uncomfortable, Andrew? Are you in pain? Is it your throat?"

A sound in the hall distracted her. A boy stood in the doorway. He was eight or nine years old, thin and dark-haired. "Are you better, Andrew?"

When I didn't answer, he came closer. "Can't you talk?"

His face was inches from mine, so close I could count his freckles. He studied me for a moment, then turned to his mother. "He looks so strange. Are you sure he's all right?"

Mrs. Tyler pulled him away from me. "Hush, Theo. Your brother's been very ill. Let him rest."

Theo's forehead wrinkled. "I hope he doesn't have brain fever, Mama. After George Foster had diphtheria, he didn't know anyone for the longest time. Father says he's still not quite right in the head and probably never will be."

"Not another word, Theodore." Giving him a gentle push,

Mrs. Tyler told him to wash and dress. "Today is Tuesday, have you forgotten? It's your turn to weed the vegetable garden."

Theo lingered just outside the door, grumbling. He'd just wanted to see me, he'd missed me, he wanted to play. My goodness, couldn't his mother understand *that*?

Ignoring him, Mrs. Tyler patted my hand. "Papa cut his business trip short when he heard how ill you were. He'll be home on the afternoon train. Won't he be happy to see you looking so well!"

Hannah came running up the stairs. "Dr. Fulton's on his way, Mama."

"He's in for a surprise, isn't he?" Mrs. Tyler smiled at me. "Dr. Fulton didn't think you'd live till morning, Andrew. The very idea — Hannah told him it would take more than diphtheria to kill you."

When Dr. Fulton arrived, he was just as surprised as Mrs. Tyler had predicted. After he examined me, he said, "If I hadn't seen Andrew yesterday, I wouldn't guess he'd ever had diphtheria. His throat is clear, his nose is clear. In all my years, I've never seen the like of it. If I didn't know better, I'd think he was a different boy altogether."

Mrs. Tyler listened closely to Dr. Fulton, but she was obviously still puzzled. Speaking in a low voice, she said, "Andrew hasn't uttered a single intelligible word. He stares so queerly you'd think he was in a room full of strangers. Quite simply, he isn't himself."

The doctor shook his head. "Fevers affect the mind in strange ways. I'm certain it's a temporary condition."

Pausing in the doorway, he winked at Mrs. Tyler. "For heaven's sake, Mildred, enjoy the peace and quiet. Andrew will be his old self in no time. Look at this as a brief respite from his mischief."

Mrs. Tyler followed Dr. Fulton downstairs. Left to myself, I wondered what they'd think if I were to tell them they were right — I wasn't the same boy, I was a totally different boy. I'd never seen them before, they'd never seen me. In fact, I didn't even exist yet. They'd never believe me, they'd think I'd lost my mind like poor George Foster.

From somewhere outside, a dog barked. A rooster crowed, hens cackled, birds sang. As quietly as I could, I eased out of bed and tiptoed to the window. The hills, fields, and woods hadn't changed much, but a narrow dirt road ran past the house instead of a four-lane highway. The front lawn was smooth and green, the bushes trimmed, the trees smaller.

Just below my window, the doctor was climbing onto a buggy seat. Hannah and her mother stood side by side, their backs to me, watching him prepare to depart. Their long white dresses billowed in the breeze. Over their heads, the leaves stirred and rustled, mottling them with shadows.

Dr. Fulton flicked a whip. The buggy creaked as the horse began to move. When he was out of sight, Mrs. Tyler walked slowly toward the house, but Hannah ran down the hill, calling to a big black dog. Picking up a stick, she flung it across the grass.

"Fetch, Buster," she called. "Fetch."

I watched the dog pounce on the stick and carry it back. Hannah held out her hand. "Give it to me, sir."

Buster shook his head and wagged his tail. He wasn't going to surrender the stick. Nothing could make him open his mouth.

Hannah laughed. "Silly old thing. Just wait till Andrew's well enough to play. He'll make you obey!"

I didn't like the sound of that. Would I be expected to order Buster around? He was at least twice the size of Binky. And his teeth — they must be enormous, as sharp as a wolf's. If he wanted a stick, I wasn't going to take it away from him. Just looking at him scared me.

But not Hannah. Dropping to her knees, she put her arms around the monster's neck and hugged him. "I expect you've missed your master as much as I have."

While Hannah played with the dog, I pondered the predicament I'd gotten myself into. As soon as Mrs. Tyler thought I was strong enough, she'd haul me out of bed. I'd be expected to act like Andrew, to know the things he knew, love what he loved, hate what he hated. Do what he did. Laugh, talk. *Be* Andrew.

It would be like acting a part in a play I hadn't read. I had the right face and the right wardrobe, but I didn't know my lines. I'd have to make them up as I went along, taking cues from the others, fumbling and bumbling, making stupid mistakes, looking like a fool.

Leaving Hannah and Buster to their game, I crept back to bed. My head ached, my body felt heavy. Weighed down with worries, I stared at the ceiling and tormented myself with new and terrifying possibilities. What if the switch worked only once? What if Andrew died after all? I'd be trapped in his life for the rest of *my* life. I'd never see Mom and Dad again, never return to Chicago, never play with my friends.

Even the possibility of escaping forever from my old enemy Martin wasn't enough to console me. I didn't want to be Andrew. I wanted to be me — Drew.

Chapter 8

Late in the afternoon, I woke to see a tall man standing beside the bed. He wore a rumpled white suit. His hair was thick and dark, his bearded face stern.

Forgetting where I was, I cowered under the quilt. "Who are you?" I cried. "What do you want?"

The man drew back in surprise. "Who the Sam Hill do you think I am?"

Hannah leapt from the rocking chair and ran to the bed. Clasping my hands, she said, "Don't be frightened, Andrew. It's Papa, just Papa."

"Papa," I repeated, "Papa." My heart was pounding so loud I thought everyone would hear it.

"He was sound asleep," Hannah said to her father. "You startled him."

While Hannah searched for ways to explain my behavior, I tried to breathe normally. Nothing had changed. I was still in Andrew's bed. The man was his father. I should have recognized him from the pictures Aunt Blythe had shown me.

Mrs. Tyler appeared in the doorway. "I heard Andrew cry out," she said. "Is anything wrong?"

"The boy didn't know me," Mr. Tyler said. "My own son was afraid of me."

Mrs. Tyler squeezed her husband's arm. "Don't worry, Henry. The fever has left Andrew weak, easily confused, forgetful. Dr. Fulton assures me a little rest is all he needs."

Mr. Tyler wasn't so sure. "There's something different about him. His eyes . . ." The sentence trailed off into uncertainty, and he turned away.

Mrs. Tyler followed him, but Hannah lingered. "I'll bring a tray up later," she promised. "I hope you're hungry. Mama fixed roast chicken especially for you." Giving me a quick kiss, she left the room.

Hours later, I eased out of bed. The hall clock was chiming midnight. In the woods behind the house, frogs croaked and crickets chirped. Otherwise, there was no sound. Wrapped in blankets of silence, the house slept.

I tiptoed slowly up the attic steps. At the top, I peered into the darkness, hoping to see Andrew. There was no sign of him. I was alone.

"Andrew?" I whispered, "Andrew?"

No one answered. I waited a few seconds and called again, a little louder this time. An owl hooted. Mice rustled under the eaves. Buster barked. But Andrew didn't come.

Afraid of waking the Tylers, I crept back down the stairs. From their round frame, the three horses watched me crawl into bed. Pulling the quilt over my head, I cried myself to sleep.

Several days later, Dr. Fulton dropped by for another visit. He took my pulse and my temperature. He examined my throat, my ears, my nose. He listened solemnly to my chest.

"Fresh air is what you need, my boy," he said.

I shook my head, but my protests did no good. In seconds, Mrs. Tyler had my nightshirt off. Sitting me up, she dressed me as if I were a floppy rag doll, too weak to do anything for myself.

Once my shoes were laced and tied, Mrs. Tyler put her hands on my shoulders to steady me. "Are you strong enough to walk?"

I gripped the bannister and started slowly down the steps. Mrs. Tyler hovered by my side, but Dr. Fulton assured her I was fit as a fiddle.

"Don't mollycoddle him, Mildred. You'll spoil him."

In the hall, I glimpsed a boy in the mirror. He wore a baggy white shirt and knee-length pants. For a moment, I wasn't sure whose reflection it was — mine or Andrew's.

Dr. Fulton opened the screen door and ushered me to the swing. "Take a seat right there, Andrew."

Without thinking, I said, "Everything looks so nice. You painted the porch and cut the grass. The ivy's gone, somebody trimmed the wisteria. But the highway, the cars —"

Mrs. Tyler and Dr. Fulton were staring at me, their faces puzzled. I shut my eyes. Just as I feared, I'd given myself away.

The swing creaked as Mrs. Tyler sank down beside me. Pulling me close, she whispered, "It's all right, dear. Things look different when you've been away from them even for a short time."

Dr. Fulton cleared his throat. "I don't know what you're up to, Andrew, but I won't have you teasing your mother. You've caused her enough worry as it is."

"I wasn't teasing." Scared to look at him, I stared at the stiff, shiny shoes on my feet. Andrew's, of course. I'd seen them in his photograph.

Dr. Fulton regarded me solemnly. "Rest," he said, "and get plenty of fresh air. Eat wholesome food, drink milk, take your tonic. And behave yourself."

After the doctor left, Mrs. Tyler went into the house. In a few moments, Hannah came outside carrying a tray.

"Milk and cookies for the convalescent," she said, "and the latest adventure of Frank Merriwell."

Hannah put the tray on a table and sat down in the swing beside me. Opening *Tip Top Weekly*, she began to read aloud. I'd already heard three stories about Frank. In each one, he was challenged to perform a courageous deed, but I always fell asleep before he accomplished it. As a hero, he was just a little too good to be interesting.

"*There was excitement at Yale,*" Hannah began. "*The sensation of the winter season had been the result of the glove fight between Bart Hodge and Buck Badger. No one had seemed to dream that Hodge could whip Badger, for the Kansan had shown that he was a great fighter, and Bart had been defeated by him in a bare fistfight the previous fall.*"

As Hannah warmed to the story, her voice rose and grew more animated. "'*I owe it all to Merriwell,*'" she read, giving the speaker an appropriate southern accent. "'*He taught me, gentlemen, that a man can be a man without always carrying a chip on his shoulder. He taught me that a man can preserve his dignity without compelling every weaker man to bow to him in humbleness. But I know that he can fight when pushed to it.*'"

Looking up from the page, Hannah sighed. "Isn't that

grand, Andrew? What a gentleman Frank is, what a lofty mind he has. Someday I hope to marry someone just like him. Trouble is, most boys around here just don't amount to shucks."

She was interrupted by a shout. Theo was running up the hill toward the house. With him was another boy, a head taller, long-legged as a greyhound.

"Oh, Jove," Hannah muttered. "Here comes Edward, the very antithesis of Frank Merriwell."

I opened my mouth to ask who Edward was, but Buster stopped me just in time. Racing ahead of Theo and Edward, the big black dog bounded eagerly up the steps. When he was close enough to smell me, he froze. Slowly, his hackles rose. Curling his lip to expose big, sharp teeth, he growled.

Sure he was going to bite me, I scooted to a corner of the swing and crouched there, taking care to keep my feet out of his reach. "Get him away from me," I yelled, "get him away!"

"Buster!" Hannah swatted him with *Tip Top Weekly*. "Bad dog!"

Theo grabbed Buster's collar. "What's wrong?" he cried. "I brought him to see you, Andrew, I thought you'd be glad."

"He doesn't look very glad." Edward leaned against the bannister, grinning as if Buster's behavior amused him. "Neither does the dog, for that matter."

Ignoring Edward, Theo murmured in Buster's ear, petted him, coaxed him to be quiet, but the dog continued to growl and then to bark. Unlike everybody else, he wasn't fooled by appearances. He knew an imposter when he smelled one.

Exasperated, Hannah told Theo to take Buster away. "I

don't know what ails that stupid dog. You'd think he never saw Andrew before."

When Theo was out of sight, Hannah scowled at Edward. "To what do we owe the honor of your company?"

Her voice was cold enough to freeze Niagara Falls, but Edward simply shrugged. "Since when is it a crime to visit the sick?"

Turning to me, he said, "From the way people talked, I thought you'd be dead and buried by now. I should've known it was too good to be true."

Although Edward made the remark sound like a joke, it was obvious he didn't like me any more than my old enemy Martin did. It was disappointing to realize you weren't safe from bullies no matter where — or when — you were.

I glanced at Hannah, but she was twisting a tendril of wisteria around one finger, giving it all her attention. Behind her, the purple flowers buzzed with bees.

Edward leaned toward me, waiting for me to say something. Instead, I inched closer to Hannah. I was onstage, the curtain was up, the audience was watching, but I was speechless. Just as I'd feared, I'd have to bluff my way through the entire performance.

Theo came back then and broke the silence. Wedging himself into the swing between his sister and me, he said, "I hope Buster doesn't have distemper."

"Maybe he's caught whatever Andrew has." Edward stared at me from under lowered eyelids. "You seem a little strange too. Not quite yourself yet."

Hannah put her arm around me. "Andrew's fine. The fever left him a little weak, that's all."

"Weak in the head," Edward added. "Like poor old George Foster."

"If you're going to insult my brother, you can take yourself off that railing and out of my sight."

Edward ignored Hannah. "Maybe we should give Andrew a little test, just to make sure the fever didn't damage his brain."

"Don't be silly." Hannah tapped the rolled magazine on her knee as if she wanted to whack Edward even harder than she'd whacked Buster.

Looking at me, Edward went on with his game. "We'll start with easy questions. What year is it?"

Hannah protested, but I answered anyway. "1910."

Edward pressed on. "Who's the president?"

"For heaven's sake," Hannah said, "stop tormenting him, Edward."

1910 — who was president in 1910? Dates, names, and faces tumbled through my head. Ulysses S. Grant? Woodrow Wilson? Chester Arthur? Arthur Chester? Teddy Roosevelt? I'd memorized the presidents for my fifth-grade teacher, but I couldn't remember them now.

"It's William Howard Taft," Theo shouted. "Everybody knows that."

"Andrew didn't," Edward said.

"Of course he did." Hannah patted my hand. "He's tired, that's all."

Refusing to give up, Edward folded his arms across his chest and grinned at me. "Let's see if you can answer this one. How many states are there?"

Without thinking, I said, "Fifty."

"Didn't I tell you he was touched in the head?" Edward laughed. "Even Georgie Foster knows there's only forty-six states."

Hannah hurled the magazine at him. "That's enough,

Edward! You know how sick Andrew's been. Lord, he was like to die."

Backing away, Edward laughed. "Don't get so riled up, Hannah. I was just teasing."

To prove it, he leapt off the railing and pulled me out of the swing. Slinging one arm around my shoulders, he squeezed so hard I was sure I heard my bones crack. "You can take a joke, can't you, Andrew?"

Before I could do more than gasp, Edward released me. Mrs. Tyler was standing in the doorway, frowning at him.

"Good afternoon, Aunt Mildred," Edward said with oily politeness. "I just stopped in to pay my respects to Andrew. I'd best be going now."

We watched him lope across the grass and vanish into the trees at the bottom of the hill.

"Good riddance," Mrs. Tyler muttered to no one in particular. To me, she said, "Come inside and rest. From the looks of you, Edward wore you out."

To Theo's amazement, I was allowed to lie down on the parlor sofa. "Today is special," Mrs. Tyler said. "Andrew's out of bed and on the mend. There's no sense in making him climb all the way upstairs just to have a nap."

Herding Theo ahead of her and beckoning to Hannah, Mrs. Tyler left me alone to rest. The shutters were closed, the room was dim. Things I'd once seen in the attic peered at me from the shadows — a stuffed pheasant under a clear dome, a pair of landscape paintings, a small organ, a glass-fronted bookcase.

The hall clock ticked steadily, insects hummed and buzzed, a mourning dove cooed sadly. Drowsy sounds, soothing, quiet, soft, but I couldn't sleep. Every time I closed my eyes, I saw Edward's face. He'd called Mrs. Tyler

Aunt Mildred. That meant he was Andrew's cousin — but who was he to me?

The heat and the monotonous ticking of the clock dulled my mind, made it hard to remember what Aunt Blythe had told me. My thoughts strayed. I found myself searching for faces in the flowered wallpaper — a young girl in a rose, an old man in a bunch of leaves. Like optical illusions, they shifted and changed, appeared and disappeared. The young girl became an old woman, the old man became a boy.

Closing my eyes, I sank into a deep sleep.

Chapter 9

That evening, I had my first dinner with the rest of the family. I was trying to do everything properly, which meant I had to watch the others and copy what they did. Bow my head for grace, use the right utensil for the right thing, pass food promptly, keep my left hand in my lap, chew with my mouth shut.

While we were eating, Mrs. Tyler told her husband about Edward's visit.

Mr. Tyler frowned. "No doubt my esteemed brother sent him to make certain the house is still standing. I hope you sent the rascal packing." He paused to take a sip of water. No one said a word. We watched him swallow and waited for him to continue. "If Ned wants to check on the property, he can come here himself and face me. I won't have that son of his pestering us."

Mystified by the anger in his voice, I glanced at Mrs. Tyler. She was leaning toward him as if she wanted to touch his hand, but the table was a good deal longer than her arm. She tapped the white cloth instead and gave him an imploring look. "Henry, please don't be so uncharitable. Think of the example you're setting."

Mr. Tyler gazed at the ceiling for a moment and sighed loudly. Without looking at any of us, he said, "Quite right, Mildred. I stand corrected." Raising his fork, he smiled at his wife. "What brought my dear brother's son to our house today?"

Ignoring the irony, Mrs. Tyler said, "He came to see Andrew, but it seemed to me he was teasing him, wearing him out with silly questions and such. When he saw me, he took off fast enough."

Mr. Tyler glanced at me. "I am all too aware that you can take up for yourself, Andrew, but if Edward troubles you, please do not solve it in the usual fashion. You know how I feel about brawling in the streets. I simply will not tolerate it."

"You needn't worry, Papa," Hannah said sweetly. "Andrew bore Edward's insults without even raising a fist. He was a perfect gentleman."

Both Mr. and Mrs. Tyler looked pleased, but Theo gave me a sharp kick under the table. "If you ask me," he whispered, "you let that bully get away with murder."

Mr. Tyler frowned at us. "Eat your peas, Theodore. And drink your milk. You too, Andrew. Good food builds strong bodies and strong minds."

Turning back to his wife, Mr. Tyler began talking about his day in court. For the rest of the meal he described his successful prosecution of a man accused of embezzling large sums of money from a bank.

No one else spoke. We ate quietly and listened to Mr. Tyler.

After dinner, Theo, Hannah, and I sat on the porch steps talking. In the darkness, I felt safe and happy. It was nice to be part of a family, to have a sister and a brother, even if they weren't mine for keeps.

Tipping my head back, I gazed at the sky. "Just look at all those stars," I said. "They're so thick and bright — millions and billions and trillions of them. In Chicago, you can't even see the Milky Way anymore. The air —"

Theo interrupted me. "What do you know about Chicago?"

Hannah's laughter saved me. "Andrew's joshing you, Theo. He's never been out of Missouri in his whole entire life."

I bit my lip so hard I tasted blood. Like a dope, I'd almost given myself away. Scared to say another word, I sat between Hannah and Theo, a stranger again, an imposter, a boy without a family. Not Andrew, but Drew.

"I wish you'd socked Edward today," Theo said suddenly. "He was asking for a trouncing."

Hannah put her arm around me. "For heaven's sake, Theo, this is Andrew's first day out of bed. Give him time. He'll get his spunk back soon enough."

Theo leaned around his sister to study my face in the moonlight. "I hope so. Before you got sick, you never let Edward insult you."

I slid a little closer to Hannah and rested my head against her shoulder. This near, I could smell the rose water she sprinkled on her face and neck. Lucky Andrew, I thought, lucky Theo. I'd have given anything to be her real brother.

"Theo's right, Andrew," Hannah said. "Edward was testing you, seeing how far he could push you. If you don't take up for yourself, matters will get worse. Think of Frank Merriwell — he never fought unless he was pushed into it, but he always defeated his foes. Frank would have despised a bully like Edward as much as I do." As she spoke, Hannah clenched her fists as if she wanted to punch him herself.

I shrank back from Hannah's fierce face. What would she think if I said I'd never hit anyone in my life? The very idea of fighting Edward scared me half to death. He was even bigger than Martin.

Needing to know more about my new enemy, I grabbed Hannah's arm. "Why does Edward hate me so much? What did Andrew — I mean, what did *I* do to him?"

Luckily, the words had tumbled out of my mouth so fast nobody noticed my blunder.

"Land sakes," Hannah said, "Edward doesn't hate you any more than he hates the rest of us."

"It's all because of the house," Theo butted in. "Isn't that right, Hannah? Grandfather left it to Papa, and Uncle Ned got mad, and now they don't speak to each other except at church."

Hannah put her finger to her lips. "Hush, Theo," she whispered. "We're not supposed to know about the will." Glancing behind her to make sure no one was listening, she whispered, "Poor Papa. It must be awful to despise your own brother."

"Uncle Ned took him to court," Theo said. "If Andrew did something like that to me, I'd most certainly hate him."

Hannah sighed and gazed at the sky. "Those stars will be shining long after we're gone and forgotten. Just think — in a hundred years, who'll care about this house? Or Papa and Uncle Ned? Or any of us?"

I stared at her. "I'll care, I'll always care, I'll —"

"Don't be silly. By 2010, we'll be dead and gone, Andrew. Strangers will be living here — if the house is still standing, that is. More than likely it'll be a pile of rubble."

"No, Hannah," I whispered, "no, don't say that. You'll live forever. And the house — I'll fix it up, I'll . . ."

But Hannah was too busy swatting mosquitoes to listen. Getting to her feet, she seized Theo's and my hands and led us to the door. "We'd better go inside before we're eaten alive."

A week passed, then another. Every night I went to the attic looking for Andrew, but he never came. In the daytime, I went on playing my part. It wasn't easy. First of all, I had to be careful not to mention things like television or radio or computers or just about any modern event. These people hadn't even had World War One yet — what would they think if I started talking about atom bombs and nuclear submarines?

The telephone was a box on the wall. It didn't have a dial. I had no idea how it worked. I knew nothing about gaslights either — when I blew one out, Mrs. Tyler was so upset she could hardly speak. I might have asphyxiated all of us, she said.

Luckily for me, the Tylers had indoor plumbing, apparently something to brag about in those days. But they kept food cold in a wooden icebox like the one my father used as a stereo cabinet. A man delivered a huge block of ice once a week. I learned to look forward to his arrival because he always gave Theo and me little pieces to suck on — a real treat on a hot day.

The Tylers didn't own a car — not many people did. The few I saw were Fords. All black. All noisy. You could hear one coming miles away.

Although the gas jet was my most spectacular mistake, I made plenty of others. Mrs. Tyler would send me to fetch something, and I wouldn't know where it was — or *what* it was. She'd ask me take a turn at the little organ in the parlor and I'd just sit there, crimson-faced, unable to play the simplest tune.

I didn't know the words to "In My Merry Oldsmobile" or "Yip-I-Addy-I-Ay" — my favorite songs, according to Hannah. I couldn't remember going to the World's Fair in St. Louis, though everyone assured me I ate so much I got sick on the train coming home and threw up in a stranger's lap. Mrs. Tyler said I was blessed to forget that as well as the time I blew up the Armigers' outhouse with a firecracker.

Everyone blamed my forgetfulness on the fever. Mrs. Tyler claimed it had left holes in my memory.

Only Buster knew the truth — I really wasn't the boy I used to be. Although he stopped barking and growling, he avoided me whenever possible. He'd look at me, his fur would bristle, and he'd walk away, stiff-legged with hostility.

One night, I went to the attic feeling more unhappy than usual. It had been a steamy-hot summer day, the kind I once spent in air-conditioned places, and I'd made one stupid mistake after another. To top it all off, Mr. Tyler had scolded me at dinner for talking with my mouth full. He wanted to know if I'd forgotten my manners as well as everything else.

The weather had put him in a temper, Mrs. Tyler said, but it hurt my feelings when he yelled at me. Dad never raised his voice, never made me feel dumb, never ranted and raved like a tyrant.

Alone in the dark attic, I broke down and cried. I just couldn't help it. I missed my parents, I wanted to go home, I was sick and tired of being Andrew.

A sudden silence made the hair on the back of my neck rise. A few feet away, a boy appeared at the top of the attic steps. Wearing my rocket-print pajamas, he stared at me, frowning and rubbing his eyes.

"Good grief, Drew," he said. "How's a fellow supposed to sleep with the racket you're making up here?"

Chapter 10

I didn't know whether to be happy to see Andrew or mad because he'd taken so long to show up. "Where have you been?" I asked. "Haven't you heard me calling you every single night?"

"Believe me, you've made enough noise to raise the dead — which I very nearly was, in spite of your modern medicine and hospitals and such."

Eyeing me glumly, Andrew sat down on a trunk. "I hope you haven't called me up here to switch places."

Taken by surprise, I stared at him. "What do you mean? Don't you want to go home?"

"Not yet, not till I'm stronger." He pulled up his pajama sleeve and showed me his arm. "See that? I'm just skin and bones. I look like death warmed over."

He shuddered at the image, but I was too upset to feel sorry for him. "I don't want to be you anymore," I said. "I want to be me, I want to go home."

"Give me more time," Andrew begged. "Please, Drew."

"You've had three weeks," I said. "That's long enough."

He fidgeted with the trunk's lock, flipping it up and down. "Couldn't we swap for keeps?"

I stared at him. "You aren't serious," I whispered, "you can't be."

Andrew huddled on the trunk, his arms wrapped around his knees, his face hidden. "What if it's my fate to die in 1910?"

"They gave you medicine, they cured you," I said. "You don't have diphtheria anymore."

Without raising his head, Andrew muttered, "I could fall, drown, be struck by lightning, get blood poisoning, catch measles, freeze in a snowstorm. There's plenty of ways to die besides diphtheria."

Andrew waited for me to say something, but I hardened my heart against him. I'd saved his life once — that was all I was going to do. Now he'd just have to take his chances like everyone else.

Finally, he raised his head and looked at me. "Suppose we make a bargain, a gentleman's agreement."

I stared at Andrew, worried by the sharp edge in his voice. He wasn't begging now. "What sort of bargain?"

He eyed me coldly. "I challenge you to a game of marbles. Ringer, to be exact. As long as I win, I stay in your time and you stay in mine. If I lose, we switch places."

"That's not fair," I said. "I don't know anything about marbles."

Andrew leaned toward me, his face pale and earnest. "It wasn't fair of you to take what belonged to me. I warned you, I said you'd be sorry. Have you forgotten?"

I opened my mouth to blame Aunt Blythe, but Andrew stopped me. "Don't tell me it was your aunt's fault," he said. "A true gent never blames a lady."

When I tried to argue, Andrew refused to listen. "We'll be like knights in the olden days," he said, "fighting for our honor."

Sliding off the trunk, he seized my hand and shook it firmly. "Meet me here tomorrow at midnight," he said.

I followed him to the top of the steps. Below was my room. I saw the electric lamp beside the bed, my posters on the blue walls, my shoes on the floor. I even heard a pop song playing faintly on the radio.

I started to run downstairs behind him, but the moment my foot touched the step, Andrew vanished, and the light went out.

"Andrew," I cried, "Andrew, come back!"

Someone gasped. Hannah was standing at the bottom of the steps, staring at me. "What are you doing in the attic at this time of night? You woke me up."

"Where is he? You must have seen him. He was right there."

"Who are you talking about?"

"Andrew," I shouted. "He ran past you. Where did he go?"

Hannah rushed up the steps. "Dear Lord, are you sick again? Is the fever back?"

She took my hand and tried to lead me downstairs. "No," I shouted. "It's not my room, it's his. I don't want to stay here, let me go home."

Hannah was stronger than I was, and in a few minutes, she had me tucked under the quilt. "Must I fetch Papa?" she asked. "Or will you lie still and behave?"

"Your father can't help. Only Andrew can, just Andrew, but he's gone, and so are the marbles. He has them."

Hannah shook me. Her face was inches from mine. "Wake up," she said, "you're dreaming, talking in your sleep."

The fear in her voice brought me to my senses. I stopped

thrashing and gazed into her eyes. "Marbles," I mumbled, "I was looking for my marbles."

Slowly, she released me. Watching me closely, she said, "You frightened me out of my wits, Andrew."

"Bad dream," I mumbled, "nightmare."

Hannah stroked my forehead. "Your eyes were so strange," she murmured. "Nothing you said made sense. It was all gibberish."

"I just wanted my marbles." I turned my head, trying to hide my tears. What would Hannah think — a boy my age crying because he couldn't find a bag of marbles.

"You're as forgetful as a squirrel," she said. "If you promise to go to sleep, I'll give you mine."

Hannah tiptoed down the hall to her room. When she came back, she was holding a bag like Andrew's. Sitting beside me, she poured the marbles onto the quilt.

"Do you know how to play?" I asked.

Hannah gave me one of her vexed looks. "Goodness, Andrew, if it weren't for me you wouldn't know the first thing about marbles. Your brain is a regular sieve these days."

I tapped my forehead to remind her I'd been sick. She looked so contrite I felt guilty. "Will you teach me all over again?"

Hannah poured her marbles onto the quilt and sighed. Without raising her eyes, she said, "Girls my age are supposed to be ladies, but sometimes I get mighty tired of trying to be what I'm not."

Cradling an aggie almost as shiny as Andrew's red bull's-eye, she cocked her head, studied her targets, and shot. The aggie hit a glass marble and sent it spinning off the bed. Hannah grinned and tried again.

When all the marbles except the aggie were scattered on the floor, Hannah seized my chin and tipped my face up to hers. Looking me in the eye, she said, "If you promise not to tell a soul, I'll give you as many lessons as you want. No matter what Papa thinks, I'd rather play marbles than be a lady, and that's the truth."

"Ringer," I said sleepily. "Do you know how to play ringer?"

Hannah ruffled my hair. "You must be pulling my leg, Andrew. That's what we always play. It's your favorite game."

I yawned. "Starting tomorrow, we'll practice every day till I get even better than I used to be."

"When I'm finished with you, you'll be the all-time marble champion of Missouri." Hannah gave me a quick kiss and slid off the bed.

In the doorway, she paused and looked back at me. "No more sleepwalking," she whispered.

When Hannah was gone, I slid the bag of marbles under my pillow. From their frame above the bureau, the three horses watched. Staring into their wild eyes, I made a promise. Sooner or later, I'd beat Andrew. Maybe not tomorrow night or the night after, but, before summer ended, I'd sleep in my room again and Andrew would sleep in his.

Chapter 11

The next morning, the minute we finished our chores, Hannah said it was time for my marbles lesson. Urging me to hurry, she whispered, "Don't let Theo see where we're going. He might tell Papa."

She ran out the back door, and I went chasing after her. The marbles clicked and bounced in my pocket, and my heart pounded in rhythm with my feet — I'll beat you Andrew, beat you, beat you, they seemed to say.

I followed Hannah under a rose trellis and came to a stop so quickly I almost tripped over my own feet. I was standing on the edge of a small graveyard. No one had told me people were buried behind the house. Maybe Aunt Blythe didn't even know they were there. Her lawn was so overgrown anything could be hidden in the weeds and brambles.

Hannah stared at me. "What's the matter? We've always played here, Andrew. Don't you remember?"

To avoid answering, I bent down to retie my shoelace. I didn't want Hannah to know I was so scared of cemeteries that I hid my face and held my breath every time I passed one.

"Surely you're not afraid of our dead." Hannah came closer.

"Of course I'm not." I tried to sound brave, but Hannah wasn't fooled.

Taking my hand, she held it tight. "You came so close to dying," she whispered. "It must make a body see things differently."

Hannah gazed at the five headstones, gathered in a group like old friends. "Grandfather, Grandmother, their son Andrew, their daughter Susan. And our sister Lucy." Her eyes lingered on the last grave, and her grip on my hand tightened. "Thank the Lord, you're not lying here beside her, Andrew."

I shivered. For the first time in my life, I knew what people meant when they said someone was walking on their grave. Little did Hannah know how truly close her brother had come to keeping Lucy company beneath the green grass.

Face solemn, Hannah brushed away a tuft of moss growing in the *L* on Lucy's stone. "You were only three or four when she died, so you don't really remember her, do you?"

I shook my head and Hannah said, "I was eight and she was ten. We both had diphtheria. We were so sick Mama thought she was going to lose us both, but Dr. Fulton saved me. He couldn't save Lucy though."

While I listened, a cloud floated past the sun and cast its shadow on the burial ground. Leaves stirred and rustled. A mourning dove called, repeating the same sad notes over and over again.

Hannah squeezed my hand. "I'll tell you a secret, Andrew. For a long time after Lucy died, I'd wake in the middle of the night and hear her breathing. I'd forget she was dead and talk to her the way I always had, whispering in the dark. She'd listen, she'd laugh. Sometimes I even felt her hand touch mine."

The mourning dove called again, and the cloud drifted away. In spite of the summer heat, I was cold. "Weren't you scared, Hannah?"

She shook her head. "Oh, no, not a bit. I was glad Lucy was near. It comforted me."

I helped Hannah pick a bunch of clover blossoms to lay on her sister's grave. When she had arranged them carefully, she said, "I fancy Lucy sees what I see and hears what I hear. As long as I live, she'll be alive too. I carry her in my heart, Andrew." She struck her chest. "Right here."

Suddenly embarrassed, Hannah leapt to her feet and ran across the grass to a grove of trees on the other side of the graveyard. Ducking under the branches, I found her kneeling in the green shade, clearing a space around her.

"If you want to play marbles, help me make a smooth place for the ring." She sounded firm, certain, in control of things again.

While we worked together to level the ground, I glanced at Hannah from time to time. Her face was calm now, but it pained me to remember the sadness I'd seen in her eyes when she spoke of Lucy's death. Thank goodness, I'd saved Andrew's life, not just for his sake but for hers too. First a sister, then a brother — how could Hannah have borne so much sorrow and loss?

"There." Hannah got to her feet and surveyed the cleared space. Picking up a stick, she drew a lopsided circle in the dirt. She scratched a cross in the middle and laid thirteen target marbles on it — one in the center and three on each crossbar. *Miggles* she called them.

Outside the circle, she drew two lines about a foot apart, took ten steps back, and drew another one. "Now," she said. "We'll lag to see who goes first."

I stared at Hannah, my face burning with embarrassment. "I don't remember how to do that," I mumbled.

She ran her fingers through her hair and took a deep breath. The first line she'd drawn was the lag line, she explained, and the one behind it was the back line. The players stood on the pitch line and aimed their marbles at the lag line. The one whose marble landed closest got to play first.

"Let me show you." Hannah eyed the line carefully and pitched her aggie underhanded. It rolled through the dust and came to a stop about half an inch from the lag line.

Hannah stepped aside. "You try," she said. "Be careful not to let your shooter roll past the back line. That's an automatic loss."

Eyeing Hannah's aggie, I threw mine and watched it roll way past the back line.

"Looks like I'm first." Hannah shot four miggles out of the ring before she missed. Sitting back on her heels, she said, "Your turn, Andrew."

I tried to shoot the way she had, but my aggie rolled feebly out of my hand. It didn't even come near a miggle.

"For goodness sake, you've truly forgotten everything I taught you, Andrew. Hold it like this between your thumb and index finger." Hannah bent my finger around the marble and steadied my knuckles on the dirt. "Now flick your thumb hard."

The aggie rolled a little farther, but Hannah wasn't satisfied. "Keep your knuckles on the ground when you shoot," she said, "and don't move your hand while you're shooting."

When I finally managed to shoot my aggie all the way across the ring, Hannah said, "Now let's play a real game. Remember, the first to knock seven miggles out of the ring wins."

While I arranged the marbles, Hannah sat on a tree root and pulled off her shoes and stockings. Wiggling her bare toes, she sighed. "Don't tell Mama. She says my feet will grow if I don't wear shoes, but I don't care if I end up wearing size thirteens. As for being unladylike — pshaw. These shoes pinch like the very dickens."

Pushing the hair back from her face, Hannah knuckled down and shot. Click — her aggie sent a cat's-eye spinning across the dirt and into the weeds.

She hit five and missed the sixth. "Drat," she muttered.

Holding my aggie clumsily, I tried to shoot the way Hannah had taught me, but it was hopeless. The miggles were scattered all over the place. I aimed at the closest, missed, and lost my turn.

"That's one of the advantages of going first," Hannah said. "You have better targets when the ring is full."

I sat back, waiting for her to shoot. Even in the shade it was steamy hot. Gnats circled our heads, humming in our ears, taking little bites.

"Try again, Andrew," Hannah said patiently.

For the rest of the long morning, we played. By the time we quit, my thumb hurt, my neck and shoulders ached, and my finger felt permanently crooked. It looked like I wasn't going to beat Andrew anytime soon.

Chucking me under the chin, Hannah laughed. "Goodness, don't look so glum. It's a game, Andrew, not a matter of life and death."

I turned away quickly and began gathering the marbles. The things the Tylers said in ignorance were downright scary.

Behind me, Hannah grabbed a branch and swung up into a tree. "Race you to the top, Andrew."

I'd never climbed a tree in my life, but I didn't dare admit it. Sooner or later the Tylers were bound to think I was a complete lunatic. They still mentioned George Foster from time to time, though never deliberately in my hearing. The Fosters had sent George to the county asylum — what if Mr. Tyler decided to do the same with me?

I took a deep breath and followed Hannah up the tree, one limb at a time, higher and higher. Leaves brushed my face, the branches swayed, but I kept going. I wanted to please Hannah, I wanted to show her I could do what she did. If she told me to jump, I would. For her, I'd fly.

When Hannah had climbed as high as she could, she said, "Look, Andrew, you can see all the way to Riverview from here. There's the church steeple and the courthouse tower."

Feeling slightly queasy, I clung to a limb and gazed at barns and houses, fields and woods, cows and sheep, the river behind the house, railroad tracks shining silver in the sunlight. It was a nice view, but all I could think about was climbing down. We were up so high — how would we ever get back to earth without killing ourselves?

Suddenly, a loud popping and banging shattered the quiet. Almost hidden in a cloud of dust, a car roared along the road below us. Cattle lumbered to their feet, horses raised their heads and galloped away, a flock of chickens scattered in all directions.

Hannah gasped. "Oh, my Lord, it's John Larkin in his father's motorcar. If he catches me looking like this, he'll think I'm a common hoyden."

Her bare foot plunged toward me. The tree swayed violently, my head swam. Afraid to move, I clung to a branch.

"For heaven's sake, Andrew, hurry. He'll be here any moment!"

With Hannah pushing me, I slid from limb to limb, down,

down, faster and faster. By the time I hit the ground, my legs were shaking so hard I could barely stand.

Without so much as a thought for me, Hannah grabbed her shoes and ran across the lawn. Her feet were bare, her shirtwaist untucked, her skirt dusty. Twigs and leaves clung to her hair. As quick as she was, the Model T was quicker. Pursued by Buster, it rolled to a noisy stop under a tree.

Without pausing to say hello, Hannah darted past John, scurried up the steps, and vanished into the house. The door had no sooner closed behind her than it opened to let Theo out. Leaping from the porch, he flung himself at John and begged for a ride. Buster circled the car, barking and snapping at the tires.

The commotion brought Mrs. Tyler to the door. "Land sakes, Buster, hush!" When the dog didn't obey, she spotted me walking slowly toward the house. "Andrew, stop lally-gagging and do something with this animal."

Obediently, I put two fingers in my mouth and blew hard. The shrill sound got Buster's attention immediately. Tail wagging, he loped across the lawn toward me. Two feet away he skidded to a stop, obviously as surprised as I was. Curling his lip, he growled softly and then slunk off toward the woods, as disappointed as a dog can be.

Too astonished to move, I watched Buster disappear into the trees. No matter how hard I'd tried, I'd never been able to make a noise like that. A pitiful little hiss of air was all I'd ever managed to produce. Yet just now, without even thinking about it, I'd blasted the dog with a whistle loud enough to wake the dead.

The idea made me shiver. Scared of my own thoughts, I turned toward Mrs. Tyler. At that moment, the world around me quivered as if I were looking at it through heat waves. The Model T vanished, the Tylers disappeared. Weeds and vines spread across the lawn. Trees grew taller. The house aged, its roof sagged, shutters hung loose, ivy covered the bricks. Andrew faced me, his eyes huge, his skin pale. Like twin statues we stared at each other, neither moving nor speaking.

I whispered his name, but when I stepped toward him, he backed away, stumbling in his haste to escape. A sound like the buzzing of locusts filled my ears. "Wait," I cried, "come back."

The next thing I knew I was sprawled on the grass and a woman was bending over me. "Andrew, Andrew, what ails you?" She put an arm around my waist and helped me to my feet. "I heard you call out. Then I saw you stagger and fall."

I tried to focus my eyes. My head ached, I was still dizzy, but the locusts were quiet. The world was steady. Andrew had disappeared.

"Should I send John to fetch Dr. Fulton?"

I shook my head, breathed deeply, tried to smile. "It was the heat, Mama. I'm all right now. Don't worry."

Keeping one arm around me, she said, "John has offered to take us on an outing in his father's motorcar, but perhaps you and I should stay home. . . ."

From her bedroom window, Hannah called, "For pity's sake, Mama, we'll never hear the end of it if you don't let Andrew come with us."

"Please, Mama. I'm fine, honest I am."

Mama sighed and reluctantly gave her permission. "But you must sit quietly. It's not wise to overexcite yourself."

I started to run toward the car, but Mama stopped me. "Wash your hands and face first, and comb your hair." As

I pulled away, she called after me, "Don't forget your neck — it's positively gray with dirt."

Alone in the bathroom, I stared into the mirror over the sink. Who was I looking at? Andrew or Drew? The boy on the lawn had been wearing my jeans, my T-shirt, my running shoes. I was wearing his clothes. I'd whistled for his dog the way he would have. I'd called his mother "Mama" as naturally as I'd once called my mother "Mom." If I stayed here long enough, would I sink down into Andrew's life and forget I'd ever been anyone else?

No, no, no. Splashing cold water on my face, I reminded myself I was just acting a part. When I won the marble game, the curtain would go down on the last act. I'd be Drew again and Andrew would be Andrew — for keeps. Till then, I'd call Mrs. Tyler "Mama" and Mr. Tyler "Papa," I'd think of Hannah and Theo as my brother and sister, I'd whistle for Buster, I'd do whatever my role demanded.

Outside, a horn blew and Theo yelled, "Andrew, hurry up or we'll leave without you!"

Yes — I'd even ride in a genuine Model T.

Chapter 12

From her seat beside John, Hannah saw me running toward the car. "It's about time, Andrew. We've been sitting here perishing of heat."

Hannah didn't look like she was perishing of anything. She'd changed her clothes and piled her hair on top of her head. Her face and hands were clean. No one would have guessed she'd spent the morning playing marbles.

Mama made room for me in the backseat, and I squeezed in beside her.

"Now don't go too fast, John," Mama said. "And be careful of the curve at the bottom of the hill. Sometimes Mr. Pettengill's cattle get out and block the road."

"Yes, ma'am." John cranked up the engine. The car shook and trembled and made a series of loud popping noises before it began to roll down the driveway, picking up speed as it went.

"Hooray!" shouted Theo. "Hooray!"

"Heavens to Betsy," Mama cried, "slow down, John. Do you want to kill us?"

Leaning over the seat, I estimated we were going all of ten or fifteen miles per hour.

"It's a good thing there aren't more motorcars on the road," Mama said. "If everyone drove like you, we'd never make it to town in one piece."

Hannah gave her mother an agonized look. "Mama," she whispered, "John knows how to drive."

Glancing over his shoulder, John smiled at Mama. "I was in St. Louis last week," he said. "I must have seen twenty or thirty cars in less than an hour. Uncle Hiram says it's all nonsense — in a couple of years, people will come to their senses and go back to a good old reliable horse and carriage. But I believe cars are here to stay."

Mama sighed and shook her head. "You'll never see my Henry driving one," she said. "He agrees with your uncle. It's a silly fad."

"How about you, Mama?" Theo bounced on the seat. "Wouldn't you like to have a motorcar?"

"Certainly not," Mama said firmly.

In Riverview, we stopped at Larkin's Drugstore for a cold drink. Leaving the rest of us to scramble out unaided, John offered Hannah his hand. Although I'd just seen her leap out of a tree as fearless as a cat, she let him help her.

At the soda fountain, Hannah took a seat beside John. In her white dress, she was as prim and proper as any lady you ever saw. Quite frankly, I liked her better the other way.

I grabbed the stool on the other side of Hannah and spun around on it a couple of times, hoping to get her to spin with me, but the only person who noticed was Mama. She told me to sit still and behave myself. "You act like you have ants in your pants," she said, embarrassing me and making Theo laugh.

While I was sitting there scowling at Theo in the mirror, John leaned around Hannah and grinned at me. "To celebrate your recovery, Andrew, I'm treating everyone to a lemon phosphate — everyone, that is, except you."

He paused dramatically, and Hannah gave him a smile so radiant it gave me heartburn. She was going to marry John someday, I knew that. But while I was here, I wanted her all to myself, just Hannah and me playing marbles in the grove, talking, sharing secrets, climbing trees. She had the rest of her life to spend with stupid John Larkin.

"As the guest of honor," John went on, "you may pick anything your heart desires."

Slightly placated by his generosity, I stared at the menu. It was amazing what you could buy for a nickel or a dime in 1910.

"Choose a sundae," Theo whispered. "It costs the most."

"How about a root beer float?" Hannah suggested.

"Egg milk chocolate," Mama said. "It would be good for you, Andrew."

"Tonic water would be even better," John said, "or, best of all, a delicious dose of cod-liver oil."

When Hannah gave him a sharp poke in the ribs, John laughed. "Andrew knows I'm teasing. Come on, what will it be, sir?"

Taking Theo's advice, I asked for a chocolate sundae.

"Good choice," John said. "You'd have to go all the way to St. Louis to find better ice cream."

While we waited for our orders, a large woman swept through the door and sailed toward us. Theo nudged me. "Oh, no, it's Mrs. Armiger," he hissed. "Now we're in for it."

As Mrs. Armiger drew near, the fountain clerk put my sundae in front of me. "Here you are," he said. "I made this one especially for you, Andrew. Plenty of chocolate sauce and whipped cream — just the way you like it."

Glad Andrew and I had at least one thing in common, I scooped up a big spoonful of ice cream. My mouth was watering for chocolate, but before I had a chance to taste it, Mrs. Armiger pounced on me. "How wonderful to see you up and about, dear boy. I was just plain worried to death when I heard you'd come down with diphtheria."

Her perfume hung around me in a cloud so dense I could hardly breathe. "Yes, ma'am," I stammered, trying hard not to cough. "Thank you, ma'am."

Laying a plump hand on my shoulder, Mrs. Armiger smiled. "Why, Andrew, I believe a touch of the dark angel's wings has improved your manners."

Theo gave me one of the sharp little kicks he specialized in. Blowing through his straw, he made loud bubbling sounds in his drink.

He expected me to do something outrageous too. They all did — the whole family was watching, waiting for me to mortify them. I could almost hear Mama holding her breath. I knew Andrew would never have sat as still as a stone, ears burning with embarrassment, but, unlike him, I couldn't think what to do or say.

"That's a very rude noise, Theodore," Mrs. Armiger said.

Mama snatched Theo's glass. "If you want to finish your phosphate, apologize to Mrs. Armiger."

Without looking at anyone, Theo mumbled, "I'm sorry."

Mama wasn't satisfied. "Sorry for what, Theodore Aloysius?"

Theo kept his head down. Trying not to giggle, he said, "I'm sorry for making a rude noise, Mrs. Armiger."

Mama gave him his phosphate. "That's better."

Theo kicked me again, harder this time. From the way he was scowling, I guessed he was mad that he'd gotten into trouble and I hadn't.

Catching my eye in the mirror, Mrs. Armiger said, "Your mother tells me you've forgotten how to play the parlor organ, Andrew."

I began to apologize, but Mrs. Armiger hushed me. "It's all right, dear. I understand." She paused to adjust her hat. "In the fall, we shall begin your lessons again. We'll get along famously this time, won't we?"

Not daring to meet Theo's eyes, I said, "Yes, ma'am."

Mrs. Armiger smiled at Mama. "I can't believe he's the same boy. Do you suppose some other child put that glue in my metronome after all? Surely it wasn't this dear angel who drew a mustache on my bust of Beethoven. Nor could he have been the rascal who climbed out my window on recital day and hid in a tree."

She squeezed my shoulder just hard enough to hurt. "No, no, no — not this sweet little fellow. It must have been some naughty boy who looked just like him."

After she and Mama shared a chuckle, Mrs. Armiger hugged me. "I believe I can make a perfect gentleman out of this child."

When Theo heard that, the laughter he'd been struggling to control exploded in a series of loud snorts. He tried to pretend he was choking on his phosphate, but he didn't fool Mama.

"Music lessons are exactly what Theodore needs," she told Mrs. Armiger. "The discipline will do him good. Suppose I send both boys to you every Wednesday afternoon?"

While Mrs. Armiger and Mama made plans, I stirred the chocolate sauce into my ice cream, appetite gone. Beside me, Theo seethed. He was blaming everything on me — the scolding, the music lessons, Mrs. Armiger. It was all my fault. He hated me.

⚬　　⚬　　⚬

Before we left Riverview, John insisted on taking our picture. "We have to preserve this moment for posterity," he said. "The Tylers' first ride in a motorcar — a memorable event if there ever was one."

Theo refused to get into the car. Sticking out his lip, he said, "I'm not having my picture taken with *him*."

He meant me, of course.

Mama took one look at my face and grabbed Theo's ear. Giving it a little twist, she propelled him into the backseat. "I've had enough for one day," she said. "Perhaps you'd like Papa to tan your hide when he comes home tonight."

Theo mumbled another apology, and Mama slid into the car beside him. Keeping herself in the middle, she made room for me.

John posed us, told us to smile, warned us to sit still, and carefully pressed the shutter of a bulky box camera. Not satisfied, he rearranged us and took several more photographs, including one of Hannah behind the steering wheel.

"The very idea — a woman driving." Mama shook her head. "Hannah has entirely too many unladylike notions already. Voting, for instance. She wants me to join those suffragettes, but if you ask me, some things are better done by men."

While Hannah defended her right to vote and drive and spit on the sidewalk if she pleased, John started the car. In a cloud of dust and noise, we left Riverview and headed for home.

As the Model T bumped over the ruts in the dirt road, I gazed silently at the fields of corn stretching away toward the blue sky. Instead of laughing and singing with the others, I was thinking about the pictures in the attic. I couldn't remember seeing a single photograph of the Tylers in a car.

Did that mean this day wasn't supposed to happen? A

little chill ran up and down my spine. Suppose what Andrew and I were doing was dangerous? Not just to him and me, but to history itself?

A tap on my knee roused me from my thoughts. "We're home," Mama said. "Are you planning to sit in the motorcar all night?"

She took my hand and led me toward the house. Theo raced ahead, calling Buster, but Hannah and John lingered by the car. Halfway across the lawn, I hung back and let Mama go ahead. Long golden arms of sunlight shafted through the trees. Birds sang. The air was so still I thought the house might shimmer and shift. Perhaps Aunt Blythe would appear and call me in for supper. Binky might race down the steps, wagging his tail, welcoming me home.

The front door opened and Papa stepped onto the porch. Buster barked and Theo laughed. The solid brick house glowed with pink light from the setting sun. Its lawn was well tended, its bushes trimmed, its roof sound, its wood trim painted. No one knew the future but me. I'd never felt so lonely, so lost, so far from home.

Behind me, John started the Model T. Distracted by the noise, I turned and watched the car rattle away in a cloud of dust.

When he was out of sight, Hannah walked toward me. Seizing my hand, she said, "You've been standing here for five minutes staring at nothing, like a regular mooncalf. Have you forgotten the way home?"

Hannah was teasing me, laughing at my absentmindedness, turning my loneliness into a joke. Without answering her, I ran toward the house, sending my shadow racing ahead to meet Papa.

Chapter 13

When I tiptoed up the stairs to the attic that night, Andrew was waiting for me. A candle illuminated the circle he'd drawn on the floor. Its flame flickered in a draft and sent big black shadows dancing across the rafters.

"Are you ready to play?" Andrew watched me sit down opposite him. He was tense, nervous, eager to begin the game. In his right hand, he cradled the red bull's-eye.

But I had other things on my mind — questions, worries, doubts. "I saw you today," I said. "You were standing in the backyard. Did you see me?"

Andrew's eyes widened. "That was you?"

I nodded, and he relaxed. "Praise be. I thought I was looking at my own ghost."

"For a minute I didn't know who I was — you or me."

"What do you mean?"

I told him about whistling for Buster and calling his mother "Mama," but Andrew just shrugged and said he didn't see why that worried me. "You're going to be me for a long time, Drew. It's best you get used to it."

"But suppose we make something happen that changes history?"

"Don't be silly. How could two boys as unimportant as we are do anything like that?" Hunching over the ring, Andrew laid out a cross of thirteen glass marbles. Each one cast a faint colored shadow on the floor.

"Did Aunt Blythe give your marbles back?"

"Yes, but it doesn't change our agreement. We play till you beat me."

I watched him aim his aggie. It spun to a stop a hair's width past the lag line. He sat back on his heels and grinned. "You won't do better than that."

As he predicted, my aggie rolled past his and disappeared into the shadows beyond the candlelight.

Quicker than I was, Andrew retrieved it. "This is my sister's shooter. Are you stealing from her now?"

"Of course not!" I glared at him, furious he'd think me capable of such a thing. "She's teaching me how to play. She's very good."

"But not as good as I am." Andrew knelt beside the ring. "Come on, Drew, no more dawdling. Let's play." Aiming carefully, he shot seven miggles out of the ring. Clickety click — one after another they spun across the floor.

"My game." Andrew dropped his marbles into his leather bag. Each click was the sound of a key locking me into his world. "I told you I was good," he said.

Trying not to cry, I stared at the floor. A tear splashed on the boards anyway, then another. Embarrassed, I knuckled my eyes with my fists, but it didn't help. I couldn't stop.

"Tarnation," Andrew said scornfully. "Don't be such a pantywaist. It would take much more than losing a game to make *me* cry."

"I know," I muttered. "You're tough and brave and you can do everything."

Andrew grabbed my shoulders. "Stop crying, stop it this minute! You must be ruining my reputation!"

Afraid of the anger blazing in his eyes, I pulled away from him. "It's not easy to be you!"

"Do you think it's any easier to be you?" Andrew followed me till I was flat against the wall with no place else to go. "At least you've studied history, you know something about how life used to be. How do you suppose it felt to wake up in a hospital surrounded by newfangled machines Jules Verne never even imagined?"

I opened my mouth to speak, but Andrew wasn't finished. "I didn't know anybody — not Aunt Blythe, not Mom, not Dad. I had no notion how to behave. What to say, what to do. I guess they thought the fever had gone to my brain. The hospital gave me test after test. Nobody could find anything wrong, so they sent me home. I tell you, it was a real shock to see everything so different."

When Andrew paused to take a breath, I jumped in with a question. "My parents were at the hospital? They came all the way to Missouri to see you?"

Andrew looked surprised. "Of course. They thought I was dying."

I pictured Mom and Dad hanging over my hospital bed, holding each other's hands, crying, promising to stay with me forever if only I'd get well. "Where are they now?"

Andrew shrugged. "They went back to their dig in France."

I was disappointed, but Andrew wasn't. Eyes shining, he said, "It must be grand to be an archeologist. Just imagine what you might find — ancient temples in the jungle, buried cities in the desert, lost civilizations under the ocean. If I live to grow up, that's what I'm going to do."

"In real life, it isn't like that," I said. "You spend most of your time swatting bugs and sifting through dirt for teeny little bits of stuff — bone fragments, shards of pottery, things like that. You'd be bored to death."

"I don't think so." Twin candles glowed in Andrew's eyes. Bending toward the flame, he blew it out and got to his feet. "If you don't mind, I'm going to bed now. Aunt Blythe has a big day planned for tomorrow. She's taking me to St. Louis to see the sights."

Vexed by his cockiness, maybe even jealous, I watched Andrew run down the steps. At the bottom, he looked back. "Better luck tomorrow night, Drew."

The next morning, Hannah said, "I believe you're beginning to show some improvement, Andrew."

I'd finally hit a marble out of the ring, and she was just as pleased as I was. The sun shone down through the leaves, dappling the ground with shadows. Hidden in the foliage, locusts buzzed and droned. Birds sang in the woods behind us. I felt good. Happy even. Right now, Hannah was all mine.

When she climbed up into the tree, I followed her. I'd done it yesterday, I could do it again today. This time, instead of going to the top, we sat on a low branch and watched the clouds drift by — bears and elephants, whales and dragons, castles and mountains, one thing shifting to another, always changing, never staying the same.

After a while, Hannah said, "I heard Papa and Mama talking last night. Mama told Papa she thinks John Larkin is fond of me."

To my annoyance, a little smile danced across her face. "I'm fond of John too," she admitted, "but Papa —"

Hannah bit her lip and frowned. "Papa said a girl with my notions will never find a husband. He told Mama I'd end up an old-maid suffragette. Those were his very words, Andrew."

Forgetting everything except making her happy, I said, "No matter what Papa thinks, you'll marry John. What's more, women will get the vote and drive cars and do everything men do, even wear trousers and run for president."

Hannah sucked in her breath. "The way you talk, Andrew. I could swear you've been looking in a crystal ball."

Clapping my hand over my mouth, I stared at her. Whatever had made me say so much? I didn't even want to think about her marrying John, and here I'd gone and told her she would, as well as revealing a bunch of other stuff she shouldn't know.

"Do you see anything else in my future?" Hannah was leaning toward me, her face inches from mine, gazing into my eyes, her lips slightly parted. "Will John and I be happy? Will we have lots of children? Will we live a long, long time?"

I tightened my grip on the branch. I was drowning, losing my identity, speaking words that made no sense. "You'll be old when I'm young," I whispered, "but I'll remember, I'll never forget, I'll always love —"

"What are you talking about?" Hannah reached out and grabbed my shoulders. "Are you all right?"

For a moment, I was too dizzy to answer. I wasn't sure who I was or where I was or what we'd been talking about. Feeling sick, I clung to the tree. Gradually, things came back into focus, the world steadied. Birds sang, leaves rustled, the branches swayed slightly. The strength in Hannah's hands calmed me.

I took a few deep breaths and managed to smile. Hannah relaxed, but she was obviously still worried. "Will you ever be yourself again, Andrew?"

"I hope so." I said it so fervently Hannah looked at me oddly. If only I could tell her the truth. She'd understand everything then. But would she believe me?

Hannah sighed and wiped the sweat off her face with the back of her hand. "I reckon the heat's enough to give anybody the fantods." She smiled at me. "Come on, Andrew, I'll race you to the pump for a drink."

Chapter 14

Hannah jumped out of the tree ahead of me and ran across the lawn toward the pump. By the time I caught up with her, she'd already filled the ladle. Tipping her head back, she let the water splash like liquid silver on her face. Before I knew what she was up to, she poured a ladleful on my head. "There," she said. "Doesn't that feel good?"

"Watch out, Andrew," another voice said. "Someone as sweet as you might melt like sugar." Theo stood a few feet away, scowling at me.

Hannah laughed and slung a ladleful of water in his direction. "Let's see what you're made of!"

In seconds, the three of us were fighting for the ladle, slopping water everywhere, turning the ground to mud under our feet, slipping, sliding, falling, laughing.

In the midst of it, Mama strode across the lawn. "Hannah, for heaven's sake! You haven't got the sense you were born with!"

Snatching the ladle, Mama whacked Hannah on the fanny with it. Next she hit Theo and me — him on the head, me on the shoulder. It stung for a second, but I was more surprised than hurt.

"Inside." Mama gave Hannah a push. "Clean up. You know I'm hosting the Women's Club in less than an hour and I need you to serve the refreshments."

Hannah groaned and rolled her eyes. "Oh, Mama, not those old hens."

When Mama raised the ladle threateningly, Hannah laughed and ran for the house, clucking at every step.

"As for you two," Mama said, looking hard at Theo and me, "I'd appreciate it if you'd both disappear for a couple of hours. Mrs. Armiger will be among my guests, and I'm not certain I can trust the pair of you."

Before she turned away, she added, "Take Buster with you. I don't want him making a nuisance of himself."

With Buster leading the way, Theo and I took a path downhill into the woods. A crow called, another answered. Like sentinels, they passed the word along — two boys and a dog were coming.

"About yesterday," I said slowly. "I'm sorry about Mrs. Armiger and all."

Theo sighed and kicked a stone. "Oh, Mama was going to sign me up for music lessons anyway."

He watched Buster bring the stone back and lay it at his feet. "I just wish you'd show some spunk, Andrew, like you used to. It's no fun getting in trouble all by myself. I could've gotten a real walloping from Papa if Mama had told on me."

I scuffed along, watching grasshoppers jump out of my way. The weeds were alive with them.

"It was that drat diphtheria," Theo muttered. "I guess you can't help it."

We walked till we came to a road. "Where do you want to go now?" Theo asked.

I wasn't sure where we were, so I just shrugged. "You pick."

"How about Trot and Owens?" Theo asked. "I have five cents — we can share a bottle of soda."

Trot and Owens turned out to be a little white grocery store with a gas pump in front. Leaving Buster under a tree, I followed Theo up the sagging steps. Inside it was dark and cool. A big fan hung from the ceiling and stirred the air round and round. Dangling strips of sticky flypaper turned slowly.

On the shelves was just about everything a person could need — clothes, shoes, food, tools, even some odds and ends of furniture in the back. It was the first time I'd been in a grocery store and I couldn't get over the prices — a hundred pounds of sugar for five dollars, a hundred pounds of salt for twenty cents.

"Look at this, Theo," I said, "twelve cents for a dozen eggs — that's just a penny apiece."

Theo stared at me. "Why, you can get them lots cheaper at Wilson's farm. Who cares anyway? Surely you don't want me to spend my money on eggs."

But I'd already moved on to something better — bins of cookies. Raisin, oatmeal, ginger snaps, all unbelievably cheap. Jars of candy too. Licorice by the yard.

"I wish I had some money," I said. My mouth was watering so hard my jaws ached.

"All we have is this." Theo showed me the five pennies, but another hand, bigger than his, swept across his palm and took the coins with it.

Taken by surprise, we stared at Edward. Neither Theo nor I had seen him enter the store, but there he was, laughing at us. When Theo lunged for his money, Edward dodged and dropped the pennies into his own pocket.

"That's mine!" Theo yelled. "Give it back!"

Edward spread his hands. "Take it if you dare."

Theo turned to me, but I pretended not to notice. Leaning over a metal cooler the size of a bathtub, I stared at the bottles of soda bobbing among the chunks of melting ice. Maybe if I ignored him, Edward would get bored and go away.

Theo heaved a sigh of exasperation and flew at his cousin, fists flying. Edward gave him a shove that sent him reeling backward into a pyramid of canned food.

The crash got the clerk's attention. "That's enough of that, you young ruffians," he bellowed. "I'll not have rowdy behavior in my store. No excuses — out you go!"

In seconds, the three of us were in the street. Theo tackled Edward again. This time, he landed in the dust at my feet.

"Do something, Andrew!" he shouted.

Buster barked, but he wasn't sure whom to attack — Edward or me. I looked at the dog, I looked at Edward, I looked at Theo, I even looked at the store, hoping Mr. Trot or Mr. Owens might run down the steps and rescue me.

Suddenly, Edward reached out and grabbed the front of my shirt. He pulled me so close I could count the beads of sweat on his upper lip. "Yes," he sneered, "do something. I dare you."

"Let me go."

Instead, Edward twisted my shirt, squeezing my neck till I could hardly breathe. "You've lost your nerve, haven't you?"

He lifted me an inch off the ground and shook me like a puppy. "How come you haven't been near the trestle all summer?"

When I made a choking noise, Edward loosened his grip on my shirt, but he didn't let me go. "All that bragging and boasting before you got sick — I knew you'd never do it. You're a lying little coward."

I glanced at Theo, hoping he might give me a clue, but he was glaring at Edward. His face was red, and the jugular vein in his neck throbbed with anger. "Andrew's not scared of nothing," he yelled. "Now that he's well, he'll do it. You just name the date!"

Edward released me so suddenly I landed on my rear end in the road. "A week from today," he said. "Twelve noon."

From where I sat, he looked enormous. Tall and skinny, long-armed, big-handed, he stood against the sky, blocking the sun, scowling down at me like the worst outlaw in any Western, old or new.

"You better be there, Andrew," he said.

"He will," Theo yelled. "And I'll be with him. So will Buster!"

The dog barked and tried to escape the grip Theo had on his collar.

Edward spat in the dust. Slowly and deliberately, one by one, he dropped Theo's pennies beside me. "I'll believe it when I see it," he sneered.

Like a fool, I sat in the middle of the road and watched Edward saunter away. When I was sure he wasn't coming back, I got to my feet. Theo saw me gather up the pennies, but, when I tried to give them to him, he hit my hand.

I looked at the copper coins shining in the white dust. "Don't you want a soda?"

"Not with that money!"

Before I could stop him, Theo picked up the pennies and flung them into the jungle of pokeberries and weeds beside the road. Buster "whuffed" and dove into the brush after them. In the silence we heard him thrashing around, looking for the coins.

"You're not my big brother anymore," Theo yelled. "You're a little crybaby! Next you'll be wearing white gloves and slicking your hair back and playing the piano at recitals like a perfect sickening old gentleman!" With that, Theo turned and ran.

Buster bounded out of the weeds, barked in my direction, and raced after Theo.

I trudged home by myself, worrying about the trestle. What was I supposed to do there? If Andrew had dreamed it up, it was sure to be terrible. Maybe I'd have to lie down between the rails and let the train run over me. Boys did that in stories, but I wasn't sure it worked in real life. It seemed to me you'd be gouged to death by things hanging from the bottoms of boxcars.

I thought a little longer. Maybe it had something to do with explosives. Andrew had blown up an outhouse once — he might want to dynamite a whole train.

I kicked a stone so hard I almost broke my toe. There was no way of guessing what went on in Andrew's fiendish mind. I'd just have to wait till tonight and ask him.

Chapter 15

When I finally dragged myself home, I was dying of heat and thirst. All I wanted was to stick my head under the pump in the backyard, but, before I had a chance to do it, the front door shot open. Buster charged outside, carrying what looked like a bunch of flowers in his mouth.

Mama was right behind him. "Come back here, you wretched cur!"

Buster never was what I'd call an obedient dog. Instead of heeding Mama's order, he ran faster. Maybe he thought it was a new and exciting game. Or maybe he was just full of devilry. What went on in his demented brain was anybody's guess.

"Stop him, Andrew!" Mama yelled.

By this time, the Women's Club was crowding out the door. Mrs. Armiger was in the lead, brandishing a parasol, her face scarlet. "Darling Andrew," she shrieked, "save my hat!"

Buster was heading straight toward me, gripping the flowered monstrosity like booty won in a war. He wasn't going to give it up. He'd die before surrendering.

From the porch railing, Theo yelled, "Atta boy, Buster! Run, run!"

Telling him to run stopped Buster. Not two feet away from me, he tore into the hat as if it were a vicious enemy. Flowers and bits of straw flew through the air. A huge artificial poppy landed at my feet, followed by a flurry of fake rose petals. It was like an explosion in a greenhouse.

Mrs. Armiger wailed, "Can't you do something, Mildred? That hat was designed especially for me by Madame Sophia. It cost over five dollars!"

Mama grabbed my arm. "Control that animal, Andrew!"

Bigger than the Hound of the Baskervilles and twice as fierce, Buster growled savagely at me. Somehow he'd managed to get what was left of the hat caught around his neck. His eyes rolled, his jaws drooled, he shook his head. Paralyzed with fear, I watched him run away, trailing flowers and ribbons and long unraveling coils of straw.

"My hat!" Mrs. Armiger shrieked. "My beautiful hat!"

"Buster," I yelled feebly. When the dog ignored me, I tried whistling again, but this time I couldn't make a sound. I guess I was trying too hard.

I honestly don't think Andrew himself could have stopped Buster. He was in a frenzy, tearing around in circles, panting, trying to shake the hat off.

Disgusted with me, Mrs. Armiger chased him, whacking his rear end with her folded parasol. Theo was two steps behind, imitating every move the poor woman made. On the porch, the other ladies huddled together, clucking to one another. One looked like she was about to faint. Another called for smelling salts.

Just then, Hannah poked her head outside to see what was going one. Her bewildered face made me laugh. I tried to stop but I couldn't. The louder Mrs. Armiger screeched, the louder I laughed. Tears ran down my face, my stomach hurt, my sides ached.

Mama tightened her grip on my arm. Giving me a violent shake, she said, "Go inside this minute! You've shamed me half to death!"

As I headed for the house, I saw Theo scrambling up into a tree. "Hooray for Buster," he called to me, "hooray for you!"

If he thought Mama wouldn't see him, he was wrong. "Theodore Aloysius Tyler," she cried, "come down from there at once. When your father gets home tonight, he'll see to you and Andrew!"

Papa found Theo and me side by side on the steps. We'd been sitting there for two hours, part of our punishment for ruining Mama's party. Now Papa was about to give us the rest of it — a whipping, Theo whispered. He was sure of it.

"Come with me." Papa's voice was soft but it hummed with anger.

Rising warily to my feet, I glanced at Theo. For once, he had nothing to say. Like condemned prisoners, we followed Papa to the back porch.

"I'm deeply disturbed by your behavior," Papa began. "At lunchtime, I ran into Mr. Trot as I was leaving my office. He told me how you conducted yourselves in his store."

When Papa paused to light his pipe, Theo inched a little closer to me, making it clear that I was forgiven. We were buddies again — the two of us against Papa.

"Edward started it," Theo muttered. "He took my whole allowance, he —"

"Be silent until you are spoken to," Papa thundered. "When I want your explanation, Theodore, I'll ask for it."

Theo hung his head.

Papa then repeated Mr. Trot's version of the events: Theo had knocked down a display of canned goods, we'd been sent outside, we'd brawled in the street like common hooligans.

"As if that weren't enough, your mother telephoned to tell me you disrupted her club meeting. You not only failed to control Buster but you laughed at his antics and actually encouraged his destructive behavior."

Papa produced from behind his back the tattered remains of Mrs. Armiger's straw hat. If I hadn't been so scared of Papa's temper, I would have laughed at the sight of it. Glowering at us both, he said, "Your allowance will cease until this has been paid for. The way I see it, you won't have a cent to spend till Christmas."

"Yes, sir," Theo and I whispered.

Turning to me, Papa said, "How often must I tell you I will not have you fighting with your cousin. No matter what Edward does to provoke you, you must walk away from him like a gentleman."

"But Papa —"

"I will tolerate no excuses," Laying his pipe on the railing, Papa unbuckled his belt. "Bend over, Andrew."

"Why?" I stared at him in disbelief. Surely Papa wasn't going to hit me.

"What do you mean, 'why?' I'm going to give you the whipping you deserve!"

Fear loosened my tongue, made me careless. "You're not my father, you have no right to touch me!"

"Don't try my patience, Andrew," Papa bellowed. "That sort of nonsense might fool Mama, but I'm not so easily deceived, my boy."

Seizing my arm, he whirled me around and brought the

belt down with a sharp whack on my rear end. The leather bit right through my trousers and stung my skin. I danced about, crying and trying to escape, but the more I struggled, the angrier Papa became. By the time he was done with me, I was sure I'd never sit down again.

Papa turned to Theo. "Your turn."

Giving me a scornful look, Theo clenched his teeth and took his whipping without a whimper. When Papa let him go, he hissed, "I don't know what in tarnation is wrong with you, Andrew. You never used to cry when Papa spanked you."

That night, I startled Andrew by striding right up to him in the attic and shoving my face close to his. For once, I was too angry to be scared of him. "You didn't tell me Papa beat you!"

Andrew raised his eyebrows. "Do you mean to say you finally earned a whipping?"

"It's not funny — he hit me with his belt!"

"Oh, horsefeathers. If Papa thought you deserved it, you probably did." Andrew studied my face. "I hope you didn't cry."

"Of course I did. It hurt!"

Andrew cradled his head in his hands. "How will I ever face Theo," he muttered. "I can't imagine what he thinks of me."

Stung by his lack of sympathy, I glared at Andrew. "My dad never hits me. Never! When I do something wrong, we talk about it. Fathers who beat their kids go to jail for child abuse."

"Truly?" Andrew smiled. "That's one more reason to keep winning — my rear end could do with a nice, long rest."

I watched him aim his aggie at the lag line. As usual, he went first. One after another, he shot seven miggles out of the ring. Click, click, clickety click, they rolled across the floor.

Andrew stood up to leave. "My game again."

"Wait." I grabbed his sleeve to stop him. "Don't go. I have to ask you something." Stumbling over words, I described my encounter with Edward. "I have to meet him at the railroad trestle next week. I'm supposed to do something when I get there, but he didn't say what. . . ." My voice trailed away. The expression on Andrew's face told me he knew exactly what I was talking about.

"Drat," he muttered. "That low-down skunk. I was hoping he'd forgotten."

Andrew hesitated. Without looking at me, he picked up a piece of chalk and started drawing a little train on the floor. Concentrating on his sketch, he said, "Before I got sick, Edward dared me to jump off the trestle."

My heart beat faster. "Is that what I'm supposed to do? Jump off?"

"Now, now, don't get all het up, Drew. It's not as bad as you think." Carefully, Andrew added a curlicue of smoke to his drawing. "You walk out on the trestle and jump in the river. Then you swim to shore. It's as simple as one two three." He tapped the chalk three times for emphasis.

My mouth was so dry I could hardly speak. Lying down between the rails or dynamiting the train might be better than this. "How high is the trestle?"

Instead of answering my question, Andrew said, "It's a test of manhood. Lots of boys have done it."

I wasn't interested in testing my manhood or hearing about other boys. I just wanted to know what was going to happen to me. Me — a boy who was scared to jump off a diving board into eight feet of crystal-clear chlorinated water.

"Is it five feet high?" I asked. "Ten feet? Twenty feet?"

Andrew shrugged. "More like fifteen, I guess, but the water's deep. As long as you don't hit a rock, you'll be fine." He looked at me and grinned. "Why, I could do it blindfolded, I could do it with one hand tied behind my back, I could — "

I flung myself at him. "Showoff! Braggart! No wonder Edward hates you."

Andrew dodged and danced away, laughing at my clumsy attempts to catch him. At the top of the attic steps, he paused for a second. "Just think, Drew — if you win a game between now and next week, I'll have to jump instead of you."

I lunged toward him, but he ran down the steps. Before he reached the bottom, he called, "Of course, I don't believe you'll beat me. Not tomorrow night nor the night after nor any other night. You'll never win, Drew, never."

"You just wait and see," I cried, but I was talking to empty air. Andrew had vanished, and I was alone.

Chapter 16

Hannah leaned toward me and touched my hand. "What's the matter? I've never seen such a long face."

To avoid meeting her eyes, I gathered the miggles we'd shot out of the ring. Half the week had passed, and I hadn't come close to beating Andrew. If I didn't win soon, I'd have to meet Edward on the trestle.

"I just can't beat him," I muttered.

"What has that dirty rat done now?"

Shocked, I stared at Hannah. Had she guessed? Did she know about Andrew and me? "He," I stammered, "he . . ."

"Drat Edward for plaguing you so." Hannah clenched her fists and scowled fiercely. "If I were a boy, I'd give him a walloping he wouldn't soon forget."

"That's more than Andrew will ever do." Theo stood on the edge of the grove. Nudging a marble with his bare toe, he watched it roll toward the ring. "So this is where you go every morning. I've been wondering and wondering."

"Don't tell," Hannah said. "Mama would take her hairbrush to my bottom if she knew I was playing marbles like a tomboy."

Theo squatted beside her. "I bet you wouldn't cry no

matter how hard Mama spanked you. Even though you're a girl, you're tougher than *some* people in this family."

"Hush, Theo," Hannah said. "You know the fever left Andrew weak. For goodness sake, you're almost as bad as Edward."

"All Andrew has to do is stand up for himself. Edward would leave him alone fast enough then." Theo turned to me. "Don't you remember what happened the time you made his nose bleed?"

Instead of answering, I practiced shooting at the miggles left in the ring. Click. Pleased, I watched a cat's-eye hop across the dirt and roll into the weeds. I was getting better and better — but I still wasn't good enough.

Hannah put her hand on mine. "Forget the marbles for now, Andrew. Theo's absolutely right. I told you before — you mustn't let Edward scare you. He's a bully and a coward. What would Frank Merriwell do if he were you?"

Frank Merriwell — I was thoroughly sick of hearing that name. "I don't care what some dumb guy in a story would do. I'm not going to fight Edward."

"Fight me then." Hannah raised her fists and danced around on her bare feet, bouncing, ducking, and swinging at the air around my head. "Pretend I'm Edward!"

I ducked a punch, and she swung again. "Put up your dukes," she ordered, "defend yourself, sir."

This time Hannah clipped my chin hard enough to knock me down. Her shirtwaist was completely untucked, her face was smudged, her hair was tumbling down her back and hanging in her eyes.

"On your feet, sir," she shouted. "Let's see your fighting spirit!"

Hannah was making so much noise she didn't hear John

Larkin push aside the branches and enter the grove. When he saw her take another swing at me, he started laughing.

Hannah whirled around, her face scarlet, and stared at John. "What do you mean by sneaking up on us like a common Peeping Tom?"

"With the noise you've been making, you wouldn't have noticed a herd of rampaging elephants." John was still laughing, but Hannah was furious.

Putting her fists on her hips, she scowled at him. "Well, now you know the truth about me. I'm no lady and I never claimed to be one. I suppose you'll start taking Amelia Carter for rides in your precious tin lizzie and treating her to sodas at your father's drugstore. I'm sure *she'd* never brawl with her brothers."

Theo and I looked at each other. We were both hoping Hannah would make John leave. Before he came along and ruined everything, we'd been having fun.

To my disappointment, John didn't seem to realize he was unwanted. Leaning against a tree, he watched Hannah run her hands through her hair. "I don't know what you're so fired up about," he said. "Why should I want to take Amelia anywhere? I've never met a more boring girl. As for her brothers — a little brawling wouldn't hurt them. Or Amelia either."

Hannah turned away, her face flushed, and John winked at me. "Your sister's first rate," he said, "but I wager I know a sight more about boxing than she does. Why not let me show you a thing or two?"

Happy again, Hannah smiled at John. "What a grand idea! But go slow, Andrew's still weak."

When John took off his jacket, I edged closer to Hannah. "I like *your* lessons," I said to her, scowling at John. He was rolling up his sleeves, probably to show off his muscles. Next to him, I was nothing but a skinny little baby. He'd knock me flat and everyone would laugh at me.

"Don't be silly, Andrew." Hannah gave me a little push toward John who had now assumed a boxing stance.

"Raise your fists like this," he said, "protect yourself."

I closed my eyes and swung at John, but he blocked my fist with his palm. "No, no, no," he said. "Slow down, take it easy, think about what you're doing."

For an hour or more, John did his best to show me the basics of self-defense. He was a lot more patient than I thought he'd be, but I was glad when he wiped the sweat from his face and said we'd had enough for one day.

"You'll never be the heavyweight champion of the world," he said, "but you should be able to duck anything Edward throws at you."

Theo wanted his turn, but John said it was too hot for more lessons. He looked up into the tree where Hannah sat swinging her feet, and smiled. "Maybe your sister will come down from her perch and offer us a nice cold glass of lemonade."

Hannah gave her hand to John and allowed him to help her. "Not that I need your assistance," she said. "I'm merely practicing my manners."

We watched John and Hannah walk away, still holding hands. "He's as bad as diphtheria," Theo muttered.

"What do you mean?"

"Diphtheria made you into a perfect gentleman," Theo said, "and John makes Hannah into a perfect lady. I'm sure I don't know which is worse — being sick or falling in love."

Without waiting to hear my opinion, Theo ran through

the burial ground, leapfrogging tombstones, daring me to catch him.

A couple of days later, John came calling again, just after supper this time. We'd set up the wickets to play croquet, and Hannah invited him to join us. He chose the red-striped mallet and ball, my favorites, and I was left with yellow, a boring color.

Brandishing a green mallet, Hannah grinned at John. "We'll take sides. You and me against Andrew and Theo."

Hannah went first. Theo and I watched her knock her ball through the first two wickets and aim for the third. She missed and stepped back to let Theo take his turn.

I leaned on my mallet and waited. It had taken me a while to understand the game, but once I learned the rules, I'd become a pretty good strategist. As soon as I had the opportunity, I planned to knock John's ball clear off the court, maybe all the way into the poison ivy at the bottom of the hill.

In a few minutes, I saw my chance. My ball rolled through a wicket and hit his. To keep mine steady, I put my foot on it and whacked my ball hard enough to drive John's into the poison ivy.

"It's dead," I crowed. "I got you!"

Hannah gave me one of her vexed looks. Turning to John, she said, "I swear he's getting more like his old self every day."

At the same moment, Buster went tearing into the poison ivy and emerged with the ball in his mouth. Wagging his tail proudly, he ran off with it. He'd lost Mrs. Armiger's hat, but he wasn't going to give up the ball. Ignoring our commands to drop it, he dashed under the rose trellis and disappeared behind the hedge.

"Drat," Hannah said. "That stupid dog must have buried a dozen croquet balls by now."

I glanced at John, hoping he'd be a bad sport. Maybe he'd say I cheated. Maybe he'd say it wasn't fair. Maybe he'd disgrace himself by refusing to play. Instead, he slapped my back and said, "Well, it looks like you'll win this game, Andrew."

Hannah glowed with admiration. Frank Merriwell himself couldn't have been a finer gentleman.

I turned away and kicked at a clump of grass. Suddenly, the air quivered and Andrew took shape beside me. In the dusky evening light, he stepped toward his sister and brother. "Hannah," he called. "Theo, it's me!"

Neither one looked up. It was obvious they didn't see or hear him. Theo went right on aiming his ball at Hannah's, and she continued to threaten him with death and perdition if he hit it.

Andrew stared at me, his eyes shining with tears, and vanished. It had happened so quickly I wasn't sure I'd really seen him.

Hannah called to me. "Stop lallygagging and take your turn. A storm's coming."

I drove my ball through the last wicket, winning the game just in time. With thunder rumbling overhead, we raced for the house, anxious to get inside before the rain started.

When I went to the attic that night, thunder muffled my footsteps, giving me a chance to see Andrew before he saw me. Lit by the candle's glow, he crouched on the floor. His face was hidden, but his shoulders shook as if he were crying.

I stared at him. "What's wrong?"

Startled by my sudden appearance, Andrew leapt to his feet, sending his shadow dancing across the rafters toward me. A flash of lightning lit his face, whitening it against the darkness behind him. For a moment, he seemed to hang in the air, as insubstantial as a ghost.

I touched his sleeve hesitantly. "You're real, aren't you? I'm not imagining you?"

For proof Andrew pinched my arm just hard enough to hurt. "You gave me a fright sneaking up here in that white nightshirt."

We gazed into each other's eyes. Overhead, wind rumbled across the roof. Rain pelted the slates.

"Tarnation," Andrew said suddenly. "I never used to be afraid of anything. Now I'm getting as bad as you, jumping at shadows, scared of the dark. I swear I don't know what's come over me."

Scarcely listening, I studied the design on his pajamas. There was something familiar about the little shapes. They had a name, but I couldn't recall it. "Those things on your pajamas — what are they?"

Andrew frowned. "Are you daft? They're rockets."

"Rockets." I repeated the word slowly, searching my memory for more information. Slowly images emerged — shuttles, space probes, moon flights, astronauts, Cape Kennedy.

Andrew picked up the bull's-eye aggie and rolled it between his palms. Without looking at me, he said, "To tell you the truth, I'm beginning to forget things too. The more I learn about you, the less I recollect about me. It's as if your memories are crowding mine out, there's no room for them in my head."

I nodded, agreeing with him. "Every day I get more like you, less like me."

"Lord A'mighty," Andrew said solemnly. "I hope that doesn't mean I'll become a total pantywaist."

110

The thought of such a dreadful fate seemed to revive him. Giving me a cold-eyed stare, he said, "We'd better play marbles while we still remember who we are and what we're doing."

As usual, Andrew went first. Confident of winning, he knuckled down and shot. Click, click, click — one after another he sent seven miggles spinning out of the ring.

"Well," he said smugly, "at least I haven't lost all my skills."

"Don't you ever quit bragging?"

"You're a poor loser, Drew. A true gent congratulates the victor."

"You were so busy congratulating yourself I didn't want to interrupt."

Ignoring my sarcasm, Andrew swung his bag of marbles back and forth, back and forth, watching the shadow it cast on the floor. His mood had changed again. "There's something I've been meaning to ask you, Drew," he said slowly. "That old man in the wheelchair — who is he?"

For a moment, I didn't know what Andrew was talking about. Old man, old man, what old man? Closing my eyes, I thought hard till I conjured up a picture — a bent figure in a dark room, face like a skull, bony hands, threatening me, scaring me.

"He's Aunt Blythe's father," I said, "my great-grandfather."

"He knows me," Andrew said. "Not you, Drew — *me*." To make his meaning clear, he struck his chest with his fist. "He knows who I am."

I remembered a few other things about Great-grandfather. "He gets confused," I said, struggling to recollect more but drawing blanks. "He can't keep people straight, he mixes up the past and the present."

"How is he related to me?"

I shook my head. Everything Aunt Blythe had told me was a jumble, a blur of relatives — great-aunts, uncles, cousins both first and second, grandparents multiplying with every generation. Untangling the branches of the family tree was too hard for me.

Andrew stared into the candle flame as if he expected to find the answer there. "Well, whoever he is, he hates me. The first time he saw me, he said, 'Go back where you belong. Rest in peace and leave me be.' "

Goose bumps raced up and down my arms. Like Andrew, I folded my arms tightly across my chest and shivered. "Stay away from him," I whispered. "He's crazy."

For several minutes neither of us spoke. We sat side by side, shoulders almost touching, and listened to the rain patter on the roof. At last Andrew stood up.

"It's almost morning," he said. "I'd better go."

I watched him run down the stairs. At the bottom, he gazed up at me, his face a pale, featureless oval in the dim light. "This evening, when I saw you on the lawn . . ."

I waited for him to go on, but he seemed to have trouble finding words for his thoughts. "Hannah and Theo." He spoke their names hesitantly, as if they sounded strange to him. "They didn't see me, did they?"

I shook my head.

Andrew's sigh blended with the wind and rain. Giving me one long, sad look, he disappeared.

Chapter 17

The next night and the night after that, Andrew beat me at marbles as usual, but he seemed to take less pleasure in his victories. Instead of boasting and bragging and carrying on like a conceited jackanapes, he began asking questions about his family — the color of Hannah's eyes, the smell of Papa's pipe smoke, the words to "Yip-I-Addy-I-Ay," his dog's name.

Although I knew those things, including every silly word of "Yip-I-Addy-I-Ay," I was beginning to forget other stuff. Chicago was a blur of noisy streets, jammed improbably with Model T's and Oldsmobiles. My apartment on Oak Street was a blank box, nothing but floors, walls, windows. When I struggled to picture my parents' faces, I saw Mama and Papa instead.

I was tempted to ask Andrew to let me win before we forgot everything, but the one time I had the nerve to hint at it, he shook his head sadly and said, "Homesick as I am, I'd rather be alive in your world than dead in mine."

The night before I was supposed to meet Edward on the trestle, Mama let Theo and me catch fireflies in the backyard. The bushes and tall grass glittered with them, more than I'd ever seen. We captured them two or three at a time. Holding them carefully in our fists, we felt their little feet tickle our hands. Green light glowed between our fingers and lit our faces.

When we'd each filled a jar, Theo and I lay down on the lawn and watched our prisoners crawl over the blades of grass we'd provided for them. Above our heads, Orion chased the Pleiades across the sky, Cassiopeia sat musing in her chair, and the Big Dipper poured stars that changed to fireflies as they fell.

Suddenly, Theo poked my side with his sharp little elbow. "You aren't worried about tomorrow, are you?"

"What do you think?"

He propped himself up on his elbows and studied my face. "You told me last spring it was the easiest thing in the whole wide world. You could hardly wait to jump. Why, even when you got sick you worried you'd die without having a chance to do it."

"I must have been a raving lunatic," I muttered.

Theo scowled, but the sound of a Model T chugging up the driveway stopped him from saying more. Its headlamps lit the trees and washed across the house.

"It's John again," Theo said. "Papa will start charging him room and board soon."

Hidden in the shadows, we watched John jump out of the car and run up the porch steps. Hannah met him at the door. From inside the house, their laughter floated toward us as silvery as moonlight, cutting into my heart like a knife.

"Hannah has a beau." Theo sounded as if he were trying out a new word, testing it for rightness. He giggled. "Do you think she lets him kiss her?"

114

I spat in the grass, a trick I'd learned from Edward. "Don't be silly."

"What's silly about smooching? When I'm old enough, I plan to kiss Marie Jenkins till our lips melt." Making loud smacking sounds with his mouth, Theo demonstrated. Pushing him away, I wrestled him to the ground and started tickling him.

As he pleaded for mercy, we heard the screen door open. Thinking Mama was about to call us inside, we broke apart and lay still. It was Hannah and John.

"They're sitting in the swing," Theo whispered. "Come on, let's spy on them. I bet a million zillion dollars they start spooning."

Stuffing his jar of fireflies into his shirt, Theo dropped to his knees and crawled across the lawn toward the house. I followed him, sure he was wrong. Hannah wasn't old enough for kissing. Or silly enough.

We reached the bushes beside the porch without being seen. Crouched in the dirt, we were so close I could have reached up and grabbed Hannah's ankle. To keep from giggling, Theo pressed his hands over his mouth.

Sick with jealousy, I watched John put his arm around Hannah and draw her close. As his lips met hers, I felt Theo jab my side. I teetered and lost my balance. The bushes swayed, the leaves rustled, a twig snapped under my feet.

"Be quiet," Theo hissed in my ear. "Do you want to get us killed?"

We backed out of the bushes, hoping to escape, but it was too late. Leaving John in the swing, Hannah strode down the porch steps, grabbed us each by an ear, and shook us like rats. "Can't a body have a second of privacy?"

Theo and I begged her to forgive us, but Hannah's dander was up. If she hadn't noticed the fireflies under our shirts, I don't know what she would've done to us.

Snatching my jar, she gazed at my captives. The flickering glow lit her face. I wanted to tell her she was beautiful, I wanted to tell her I'd love her forever, but all I could say was "These are for you, I caught them just for you, Hannah."

"Poor things," she said softly, her temper gone without a trace. "I'll have to let them go, Andrew. They'll die if I don't."

Before I could stop her, she removed the lid and held the jar high over her head. "Fly away, fly away," she cried. Like sparks from a bonfire, the fireflies escaped in a sparkling green mist.

Theo handed his jar to Hannah. "Set mine free too."

In moments, Theo's fireflies rose and scattered across the dark sky.

"They're going to the moon," Theo shouted. "They're going to the stars!"

"I wish I could send the pair of you with them," Hannah muttered. "Maybe I'd have some peace and quiet then."

We crossed the dew-soaked grass and climbed the front steps. Theo darted into the house, but I sat on the railing near the swing. There was a pitcher on the table, and I was hoping Hannah would offer me some. *I* lived here, John didn't. Surely I had a right to a glass of that lemonade.

From the shadows, John smiled at me, but I pretended not to notice. Hannah was sitting beside him. A little too close, I thought. Surely Papa wouldn't approve.

"Have you been practicing your boxing?" he asked.

116

I nodded but I kept my eyes on the huge moth fluttering against the window screen. Plock, plock, plock — it wanted to get to the light in the parlor.

"It sure is hot," I said. "A glass of lemonade would really taste good."

Hannah laughed. "Andrew is known all over Riverview for his subtlety."

I scowled at her, angered by the simpery way she spoke to John, but Hannah just laughed again. "Run along, Andrew. It's way past your bedtime."

"Yes," John agreed. "Growing boys need their rest."

Before I could think of a fitting reply, Mama appeared in the doorway. "Stop pestering your sister, Andrew," she said. "It's time you were upstairs in bed."

I looked at Hannah, hoping she'd rescue me, but all she said was, "Good night, Andrew."

John raised his hand in a farewell gesture, and at the same moment, Mama stepped outside and collared me. "When I tell you to do something, I expect to be obeyed." Giving my bottom a swat, she sent me upstairs.

Theo was waiting in the hall. Puckering his lips, he threw his arms around me. "Oh, John, John," he squealed. "Kiss me, darling, kiss me."

While we scuffled, Papa's voice rolled up the steps like thunder. "Stop the horseplay, boys, and go to sleep!"

Scared to risk a whipping, Theo and I sprang apart and ran for our beds. Under my pillow, the hard lump of the marble bag reminded me I'd soon climb the attic steps. If I beat Andrew, I'd be safe from Edward, but I'd never see Hannah and Theo again. For the first time, I felt a pang of regret at the thought of returning to my own world.

o   o   o

I needn't have worried. Although I won the first turn, my fourth shot went wide of its target. Aiming carefully, Andrew knocked out six before he missed.

"I can't believe this," he said glumly. "If I keep getting worse and you keep improving, you may beat me after all."

Holding my breath, I shot my aggie at one of the four marbles left. To win, I had to knock all of them out of the ring, not an easy feat. Thinking of rockets and TV's and computers and other things I couldn't remember the names of, I watched my shooter roll right past my first target.

"My turn." Andrew picked up his bull's-eye and sent a cat's-eye spinning across the floor. He sighed and sat back on his heels. "That's seven. I win again."

Too disappointed to speak, I watched Andrew tighten the knot on his bag of marbles. His face was calm, his fingers deft, his body relaxed. Raising his head, he looked at me. "Is tomorrow the day you meet Edward?"

"You know perfectly well it is." Giving in to my temper, I leapt to my feet and kicked the remaining marbles so hard they scattered in all directions. "It's not fair. *You* should be jumping off that trestle, not me!"

Andrew's eyes widened. "I told you, there's nothing to be scared of."

"Prove it," I yelled. "Switch places with me — be yourself for just one day. If you jump, I'll do anything you want, I swear I will. I'll be you forever if I have to."

Andrew backed away. "We made an agreement," he whispered, "a gentleman's agreement. It would be dishonorable to break it."

"Twenty-four little hours," I begged, "that's all I'm asking."

"I can't risk it."

I stared at Andrew, shocked to see a tear run down his cheek. Wiping his face with his pajama sleeve, he said, "Don't you see? I don't dare jump. If I'm doomed to die in 1910, I'll drown in the river, I know I will."

A gust of wind blew the candle out. In the sudden darkness, I heard Andrew run downstairs. By the time I reached the top of the steps, he was gone.

Chapter 18

The next morning, Hannah found me in the porch swing, rocking glumly back and forth.

"I was waiting for you in the grove," she said. "Don't you want to play marbles?"

I shook my head. What was the use? In a few hours, they'd be fishing my body out of the river. "Theo and I are going somewhere in a little while," I told her.

She sank down beside me and fanned herself with an old *Tip Top Weekly*. "Whew. Only ten o'clock, and already it's as hot as an oven out here."

I glanced at Hannah sitting there so innocently. It would break her heart to lose me, she'd said so herself. If I told her the truth, maybe she wouldn't be so sad when I drowned. She'd know her true brother was alive and well in another time.

Clearing my throat to get her attention, I said, "I really am a different boy."

Hannah took my confession as a joke. "At first you acted so strange I truly found myself wondering about you. But not anymore — every day you act more and more like your old self."

"You don't understand," I said. "Let me finish —"

Without giving me a chance to explain, Hannah got to her feet and headed toward the door. "No more jokes, Andrew. I have to help Mama with the canning." Hannah ran her hands through her hair, lifting its weight off the back of her neck. "Drat those peaches. Why can't they wait till cool weather to ripen?"

The screen door slammed shut, leaving me with a mouthful of revelations. Not that it mattered — she wouldn't have believed me anyway. Picking up *Tip Top Weekly*, I fanned myself vigorously, but it didn't do a speck of good. The air was just as hot as ever.

All too soon, Theo came looking for me. "It's after eleven. Time to go, Andrew."

Reluctantly, I laid the magazine aside and followed him down the porch steps. Halfway across the lawn, Buster spotted us. When Theo saw him, he whistled and the dog dashed toward us, barking and wagging his tail, glad to be included on an outing. He actually nuzzled my hand and grinned at me. In a way it scared me more to see him getting so friendly. Who did he think I was?

Before I plunged downhill behind Theo and the dog, I looked back at the house. Its windows sparkled like fire in the sunlight. Hannah waved from the back porch. As I raised my hand, the scene quivered. Andrew appeared in his sister's place. He gazed at me, his face solemn. "Good luck, Drew," he called.

Ahead of me, Theo yelled, "Hurry, it's almost noon."

Andrew vanished. The porch was empty. The dish towel Hannah had been holding hung on the railing, a bright splash of color.

At the bottom of the hill, Theo waited impatiently.

Nearby, Buster snuffled through the bushes, looking for rabbits. Crows cawed in the woods, jays scolded. Sunlight dappled the bushes and trees. I smelled honeysuckle and damp earth.

Light-headed, I ran down the path, ducking branches, stumbling on roots, skidding on loose stones. I reached Theo's side, weak-kneed and gasping for breath.

Theo stared at me. "You've got the oddest look on your face, Andrew."

I forced myself to breathe normally. My heart slowed, my knees stopped shaking. "What do you mean?"

He studied my features for a few seconds, concentrating so hard his forehead wrinkled. "You're just plain Andrew now," he said, "but a minute ago, when you came running down the hill, you looked different."

As perplexed as Theo, I pressed my hands against the sides of my head and tried to keep my identity from slipping away. Was I Drew or Andrew? I wasn't sure anymore. His time and mine flickered back and forth like images in an optical illusion.

Theo touched my arm. "Come on, Andrew. Edward will think we're not coming."

Silently, I followed him down the path into the woods. The mossy ground was cool under my bare feet, but even in the dense green shade, the heat clung as close as a second skin. The air was heavy with humidity. Clouds of gnats circled my head. Mosquitoes whined in my ears and bit right through my clothes.

We walked single file, slowly, silently, swatting insects and ducking low branches. Buster first, then Theo, then me. And Andrew — I looked over my shoulder, expecting to see him close behind, treading on my heels, merging his personality with mine, becoming part of me. I stumbled and tripped, bushes lashed my face, my head ached as if someone were drilling a hole through my temple.

Suddenly, we were out of the woods. The trestle was just ahead, a high iron bridge spanning the river, at least twenty feet above the water. I couldn't imagine jumping from something that high and living to tell about it.

"Come on, Andrew." Theo was already halfway up the embankment, looking back at me. Above him, Edward stood silently, arms folded across his chest, waiting for us.

It was a steep climb, made treacherous by cinders, loose stones, and broken glass. By the time I reached the top, I was out of breath.

"So you showed up after all," Edward said. "I didn't think you'd have the intestinal fortitude."

I looked to the right and to the left. Shimmering in the heat, the tracks vanished into the woods on either side of the trestle. "What if a train comes?"

"You know as well as I do there's only two a day," Edward said. "One in the morning and one in the evening."

"That's right," I mumbled, "I forgot."

Gripping my shoulder, Edward said, "Let's go. We're wasting time."

Utterly fearless, Theo ran ahead, jumping from tie to tie as if he didn't notice the empty spaces between them. Buster followed a little more cautiously, head down, watching his step.

Weak-kneed with terror, I stepped onto the trestle. There was no railing, nothing to keep me from falling. At any minute, I expected to slip between the ties and plunge into the river.

In the middle, Edward leaned over and spit. "This is just

about where Emmet Burden drowned. He landed on that rock."

We all stared at the boulder just below the water's surface. Sparkling in the sunlight, the river swept over its broad back.

"I was there when they found him," Edward said. "Have you ever seen a body that's been in the water for a week? The fish eat your eyes, they chew your nose off, they bite your fingers and toes and take chunks out of your skin. Emmet looked like swiss cheese."

I gagged, but Theo said, "Andrew knows where to jump. Lester Jones showed him."

"I've never been on this bridge," I said, but even as I spoke I wasn't sure. Doubts filled my head. Maybe Theo was right, maybe I'd just forgotten. Clenching my teeth, I swallowed hard. No, no, it was Andrew who'd been here before, not me. It was Andrew who'd said he'd jump, Andrew who should be here now. Not me, not me, not me.

"What are you talking about?" Theo asked. "Don't you remember *anything*?"

The river's dull roar filled my ears, my forehead pounded with heat, the sharp smell of creosote burned my nostrils. Afraid to sit, afraid to stand, afraid to move, I stared down at the water. Fate demanded a death. Mine or Andrew's — what difference did it make?

"Well, what are you waiting for?"

I looked at Edward. The sun was behind him, shining in my eyes. He was a dark shape blocking the light.

"You little braggart," he said. "Lies, lies, lies — I knew you wouldn't jump."

I backed away, but Edward came closer. "Show me how brave you are."

He pushed me just hard enough to make me stagger.

Under my feet, the railroad tie was hot, splintery, oozing tar, but I clung to it with my bare toes.

"You're making a big mistake," I whispered. "I'm not Andrew, I'm Drew."

The sound of the river drowned my words. Neither Theo nor Edward heard me.

"Hit him," Theo yelled at me. "Knock him in the water!"

"Stay out of this," Edward shouted.

"Nyah, nyah, nyah — you can't get me!" Theo stuck out his tongue and danced away from his cousin.

Red-faced with anger, Edward lunged at Theo. Maybe the sun was in his eyes, maybe he was too mad to be careful, but he lost his balance. Waving his arms wildly, he reached for me, missed, and fell off the trestle. Down, down, down he plummeted, his face turned up to us, his mouth open in a silent scream.

The water closed over Edward so quickly it took a moment for me to realize he'd actually fallen. One second he was standing beside me. The next second he was gone. How had it happened so fast?

Far below, the river slid past, its skin unbroken, so brown with mud I saw my shadow on its surface. What had Andrew and I done? We were the guilty ones, not Edward. He wasn't meant to die.

Suddenly, Edward's head emerged from the water. He waved his arms, cried out, struggled against the current, sank again.

"Edward can't swim worth shucks," Theo whispered. "If you don't help him, he'll drown for sure." Eyes blank with fear, he stared at me, waiting for me to act. I was his big brother, I knew everything, surely I wasn't going to stand by and let this happen.

Dizzy with fear, I asked myself what Andrew would do.

Stories from *Tip Top Weekly* flashed through my mind. Like his hero Frank Merriwell, Andrew wouldn't hesitate. No matter how much he detested his cousin, he'd jump into the river and save him.

Well, I'd taken Andrew's place, hadn't I? I had no choice but to do what he'd do. Taking a deep breath, I closed my eyes and leapt off the trestle.

Chapter 19

I fell through the air, faster and faster, and hit the water feet first. Down, down I plunged, straight to the mud at the bottom. The river was dark and cold. Strong currents tugged at my legs. The branches of a sunken tree snagged my shirt and held me with bony fingers. My heart pounded, my lungs ached. Kicking hard, I pulled free and swam up toward the light.

When I surfaced, I saw Edward several yards away, bobbing along, still struggling. I swam toward him, but he sank before I reached him. Taking a deep breath, I dove after him, but the water was so murky I couldn't even see my own hand.

I rose again. No sign of Edward this time. The river roared in my ears and foamed around me, smelling of decay. Too tired to fight it, I let the current carry me until I spotted Edward again. I floundered toward him and grabbed his shirt. Getting a good grip on his shoulder, I used the last of my strength to tow him to a tree trunk lodged between a couple of rocks.

Exhausted, we clung to the branches. Above the noise of the water, I heard Edward gasping for breath. His lips were purple with cold, his face was dead white. Like me, he was shivering.

From the trestle, Theo shouted, "I'm coming, Andrew. Wait right there!"

"Don't jump!" I yelled. "Climb down the rocks."

A snort from Edward drew my attention back to him. "Poor little Andrew — did you fall in the cold, cold water too?" His voice was loaded with sarcasm.

"Didn't you see me jump?"

Edward narrowed his eyes, increasing his resemblance to a rat. "Bull feathers. You fell, just like I did."

I shook my head. "I thought you were drowning, I was trying to save you."

"Don't make me laugh. I wasn't in any danger."

Stunned by his ingratitude, I watched Edward haul himself onto the rocks. Water streamed from his shirt and trousers. Getting to his feet, he said, "Even if I had been, I doubt a little pantywaist like you could have helped matters."

Turning his back, he started to walk away.

An anger I didn't know I possessed raged through me. Scrambling after Edward, I grabbed his arm and made him face me. "How dare you be so ungrateful?" I shouted. "I risked my life to save you! A true gent would at least say thank you!"

I was as astonished as Edward. Had I spoken? Or had Andrew? Part of me wanted to apologize, take the words back, turn and run, but the other part was in control. Clenching my fists, I raised them the way John had taught me.

Edward backed away. I stepped closer, dukes up, ready to defend myself.

128

"You lay a hand on me and I'll tell my father," Edward said.

Sure it was a trick, I danced around him on my toes, eager to try one of John's punches. I wanted to make Edward's nose bleed, I wanted to give him a black eye, I wanted to knock him flat.

"I'll say you pushed me off the bridge," Edward yelled. "I'll say you almost made me drown."

I kept my guard up. Edward wasn't going to distract me with empty threats. I was Andrew, boy champion. I'd make Theo proud of me. I'd make Hannah glow with admiration. I'd show them all — even John. Like Frank Merriwell, I'd been pushed far enough.

Suddenly, Edward bent down, picked up a handful of river sand, and hurled it in my eyes. Half-blinded, I flung myself at him. We rolled on the ground, grappling and yelling. While we struggled, Buster ran around us, barking. I hoped he was on my side, but I couldn't be sure. For all I knew he'd decide to take a chunk out of me.

As things turned out, it wasn't Buster who bit me — it was Edward. When I felt his teeth sink into my shoulder, I hauled off and punched him so hard I thought I'd broken my hand.

That was all it took. Squirming away from me, Edward scrambled to his feet. His nose spouted blood. "Your father will hear about this," he hollered.

With Buster snarling and snapping at his heels, Edward plunged into the woods. Dazed, I sat on the ground and listened to him crash through the underbrush.

By the time Buster came back, Theo had made his way down from the trestle. Crouching beside me, he touched my left eye reverently. "You're going to have a beaut of a shiner."

I stared at my fists in disbelief. Were they mine or Andrew's? The hot sun beat down on my head, the coarse grass scratched the back of my legs. Nearby, the river rumbled and droned. Crows cried in the woods. I'd hit Edward, I'd made him cry and snivel and threaten to tell, I'd chased him away. Me — Drew. Or me — Andrew?

"You really showed Edward," Theo was saying. "It was like old times. He won't bother us again, I wager."

Theo flopped down on his back in the grass and grinned at me. Exhausted, I stretched out beside him. Buster dropped to his haunches and panted happily into my face.

Gazing into his yellow eyes, I asked the dog a silent question. *Who am I?*

Buster wagged his tail and licked my nose. I shook my head. "You're wrong," I whispered, "I'm not Andrew."

Theo turned his head drowsily. "What did you say?"

"Nothing." While the sun dried my clothes, I watched clouds shape and reshape themselves. An hour passed, maybe more. Theo was so quiet I guessed he'd fallen asleep. I was tired too, but every time I closed my eyes I saw Edward falling, I saw the river closing over him. Whether he'd admit it or not, I'd saved his life.

Or had I? I wasn't really sure who had jumped off the trestle — Andrew or me.

On the way home through the woods, Theo kept up a constant chatter about the fight, exaggerating it beyond all recognition. Weary of the sound of his voice, I interrupted him. "What if Edward tells his father? What will Papa do?"

Theo's eyes traveled from my swollen eye to my torn shirt. His lip quivered. "We'll get the beating of our lives."

I swallowed hard. "But you didn't do anything. I was the

one who jumped in the river, I was the one who fought Edward. I'll take full responsibility."

Theo kicked at a stone. "It won't matter to Papa. I was with you. That'll be enough for him."

We were almost home. On the hill above us, the house was a tall, dark shape silhouetted against the sunset. I wished I could make time race ahead, but nothing shifted, nothing shimmered. I didn't see Aunt Blythe, I didn't see Andrew, just Hannah running down the path to meet us.

"Papa's in a real temper," she said. "What have you two done now?"

"Edward told on us," Theo whimpered. "We're going to get a whipping, Andrew."

Hannah stared at my eye. "Have you been fighting with Edward?"

For a moment, Theo forgot Papa. "You should've been there, Hannah." He clenched his fists and swung at the air. "Pow! Bam! Biff! Andrew punched the living daylights out of Edward. He made his nose bleed, he —"

The sound of Papa's voice stopped poor Theo in mid-sentence. Belt in hand, he stood on the porch waiting for us. "Step lively," he called. "The longer you keep me waiting, the angrier I become."

Mama laid her hand on Papa's arm. "Please don't be too hard on them. Andrew's health is still precarious, and Theo's merely a child."

Hannah squeezed my shoulder. "Be brave," she whispered before she followed Mama into the house.

Brave, I thought, *brave* — yes, I was as brave as Andrew now. I'd jumped off the bridge. I'd fought Edward. This time, I'd take my whipping without crying.

Papa frowned at me. "Ned tells me you dared Edward

to jump from the trestle. When he refused, you pushed him into the river and then fought him like a savage. Is this true?"

"It was an accident, sir. Edward lost his balance and fell. I thought he was drowning, so I jumped in after him."

"And the fight?"

"Edward insulted me. I lost my temper."

Papa turned to Theo. "Do you agree with your brother's account of the incident?"

"Yes, sir," Theo said. "Edward is a liar and a bully and a coward. He's the one who should be whipped, not Andrew and me."

"That's enough, Theodore." Papa paced back and forth as if he were in court. "Although bad enough in itself, it is not the fight alone that displeases me. After Emmet Burden drowned, I forbade you to go to the trestle. I presume you both remember my proscription?"

Even though I didn't, I knew better than to say so.

"Yet you went there anyway."

"Yes, sir."

For a few moments, Papa rested his case. Swinging his belt against his palm, he considered Theo and me. With each slap, my heart beat faster.

"To summarize," he said at last, "you disobeyed me. First, you endangered your lives on the trestle. Secondly, you fought with your cousin a week to the day after I punished you for the same offense. I told you then and I tell you now, I will not tolerate such behavior."

Papa took a deep breath. "Bend over, Andrew."

I clenched my teeth and shut my eyes. Gripping the railing so hard my knuckles turned white, I took six lashes without flinching or shedding a tear.

After Papa finished with Theo, he slid his belt back into his trousers. "Stay off the trestle, both of you. And avoid your cousin. I don't enjoy these punishments any more than you do."

"Yes, sir," we said.

"Now, wash your hands and make yourselves presentable," Papa said. "Dinner will be served in five minutes."

At the table, Mama heaped mashed potatoes on Theo's and my plates. She also made sure we had the best slices of tomato and very few lima beans.

Papa frowned. "You know the importance of discipline as well as I do, Mildred. Boys must not be coddled."

But I noticed he gave Theo and me the drumsticks he usually reserved for himself.

While Papa talked about his day in court, I relived my fight with Edward. What a lousy, stinking, ungrateful coward he was. Hateful. Underhanded. Sly and dishonest. A tattletale. What branch of the family tree had produced a rotten apple like him?

A creaking noise in the hall distracted me. I looked up from my plate. An old man in a wheelchair scowled at us from the doorway. "What are you doing here?" he asked. "Get out, all of you. This is my house now."

I jumped up from my chair. "Great-grandfather," I cried. "You're, you're —"

The room spun, and Edward vanished. To keep from falling, I gripped the table. My glass tipped over. A stream of water ran across the cloth.

Mama caught me in her arms. "Help me, Henry," she cried, "the boy's about to faint."

Movement, voices, lights — everything blurred and ran together. Clinging to Mama, I sank into a well of darkness.

Chapter 20

I woke up hours later. Downstairs, the clock was striking twelve. Midnight — time to do something. I gazed at the ceiling, trying to remember what it was. Overhead, the attic floor creaked, groaned.

Andrew — it was time to meet Andrew.

Slowly, I eased out of bed. My knees were weak, my head ached, nothing seemed solid — not even the floor beneath my feet. I felt as insubstantial as the moonlight slanting through the windows.

The first thing Andrew said was "What happened at the trestle?"

"Edward fell," I said. "He almost drowned."

Andrew grinned. "It's a pity he didn't."

It was no joke to me. Suddenly angry, I leaned toward him. "Do you know who Edward is?"

Startled, Andrew backed away from me. "Of course I do. He's my cousin, you nincompoop."

"He's also Aunt Blythe's father. He's Dad's grandfather. He's *my* great-grandfather."

Andrew's eyes widened. "Are you telling me Edward is the old man in the wheelchair?"

"Yes."

"Is that right?" Andrew shook his head. "Lord A'mighty, I never would have guessed. He must be close to a hundred years old. That means —"

Still mad, I interrupted Andrew's speculations. "If my great-grandfather had died when he was twelve, where do you suppose I'd be?"

I paused a moment to let him think about it. Then I said, "I wouldn't exist, Andrew — neither would Dad or Aunt Blythe!"

He hugged his knees close to his chest and stared silently at the candle. It was a tiny stub of wax now, barely big enough to give any light.

"What we're doing is dangerous," I said. "Things are happening that weren't supposed to — like Edward almost drowning."

Without looking at me, Andrew shifted the marbles around, making new patterns in the ring. Although his face was hidden, I saw a tear hit the floor, then another.

"You've given me a whole summer, Drew," he said sadly. "Maybe it's time to go home now and take my chances like everybody else."

"Do you mean you give up?" I stared at him, more disappointed than I'd believed possible. "We don't have to play ringer anymore?"

Andrew raised his head and scowled at me. "Of course I'm not giving up! Just because I cried doesn't mean I'm a pantywaist coward like you."

Getting to his feet, Andrew toed the pitching line. "We'll lag as usual," he said. "Don't think I intend to lose either. You have to beat me fair and square, those are the rules."

Andrew aimed his aggie carefully. It rolled to a stop half

an inch past the lag line. Holding my breath, I threw mine after his. It landed a hair closer.

"You go first," Andrew said.

I'd shot three marbles out of the circle when a sound startled me. Hannah was standing at the top of the steps, staring at me. "Andrew, what are you doing out of bed? You're ill, you need to rest."

I crouched beside the ring, speechless with surprise, but Andrew jumped to his feet. "Hannah," he cried, "Hannah."

Although he was right in front of her, Hannah didn't see her brother. She walked through him as if he didn't even exist.

"I've been lying awake worrying about you," she said to me. "When I heard noises, I thought you and Theo were up here. But you're all alone."

Andrew clung to his sister. "He's not alone, I'm with him. Look at me, Hannah, please look at me."

Unaware of anything but the cold, Hannah shivered. "Lord," she whispered, "I'm freezing. You'll catch your death in this draft, Andrew."

When I neither spoke nor moved, Hannah dropped to her knees and gazed into my eyes. "You're in a trance," she whispered. "For heaven's sake, wake up."

Finding my voice at last, I said, "Can't you see him?"

"See who?" Pale with fright, Hannah stared at me.

I pointed at Andrew. "He's standing right in front of you!"

"Have you taken leave of your senses?" Hannah grabbed my shoulders and shook me. "There's no one in this attic but you and me."

Andrew was crying now, hanging on to his sister, begging her to see him. But Hannah was too scared by my behavior to see or hear anything but me. Deaf to Andrew's sobs, she pulled me to my feet. "You must go back to bed."

"No," I shouted. "Not yet! I have to finish this game." I couldn't leave Andrew, not now, not when I was finally winning.

Hannah released me so suddenly I staggered backward. "I'll fetch Papa!" she cried.

Andrew threw himself at her. "Hannah, stop, you're ruining everything!"

I grabbed his arm. "Let her go. We don't have much time!"

Casting a last terrified look at me, Hannah ran downstairs, calling for Mama and Papa.

Andrew turned to me, his face streaked with tears. "Quick, Drew. Shoot four more marbles out of the ring!"

Holding my breath I aimed. Click, click, click. An immie, a cat's-eye, and a moonstone spun across the floor, but I missed the fourth.

Andrew knuckled down and shot at the scattered marbles. Of the seven in the ring, he managed to hit two before he missed.

Downstairs I heard Hannah pounding on Papa and Mama's door.

"One more, Drew," Andrew whispered.

It was hard to aim carefully. Papa and Mama were awake. Their voices rose as Hannah tried to explain I was in the attic acting as if I'd lost my mind. My hand shook and the first marble I hit merely clicked against another.

Andrew took his turn, hit three, and missed the fourth. "Send me home, Drew," he begged. "I don't care if I die when I get there."

Two marbles were left — a carnelian and an immie,

widely separated. Neither was close to my aggie. Even for someone as good as Andrew, it was a hard shot.

Holding his breath, Andrew crossed his fingers and closed his eyes.

I knuckled down and aimed for the carnelian. Click. As Papa tramped up the steps with Mama at his heels, the seventh marble rolled into the shadows. My aggie stayed in the middle of the ring.

Andrew let out his breath and stared at me. I'd won — what would happen now?

Chapter 21

"What's the meaning of this?" Papa strode toward us. "You've disturbed the entire household, Andrew."

Mama gripped his arm. "For goodness sake, Henry, don't frighten the child. Haven't you done enough damage? I told you not to whip him!"

Papa made an effort to calm down. Taking a deep breath, he squatted in front of me. "What's troubling you, son?" he asked. "Surely a spanking didn't cause this."

Aching with sadness, I put my arms around his neck. I'd won, I'd finally beaten Andrew. I'd thought I'd be happy, but I wasn't. "I don't want to leave you and Mama," I sobbed.

Papa held me tight. "Now, now," he said. "Where did you get such a silly notion? You aren't going anywhere."

While Papa comforted me, Andrew climbed onto his father's shoulders, piggyback style. No one saw him but me. No one heard him say, "Hush Drew, you're shaming me in front of everyone."

Ignorant of Andrew's presence, Papa shivered. "Fall's coming. Feel the nip in the air?"

Hannah and Theo were waiting for us at the bottom of

the steps. "Mama," Theo whispered, "is Andrew sick again?"

Mama shook her head, but Theo looked unconvinced. Slipping his hand in Hannah's, he watched Papa lay me on my bed.

On the other side of the room, Andrew took a seat in the rocking chair. It was obvious he didn't enjoy being invisible. Staring at Hannah and Theo, he rocked the chair vigorously. When that didn't get their attention, he sang "I've Been Working on the Railroad" at the top of his lungs. But no matter what he said or did, he couldn't make his sister or his brother see or hear him.

I knew Andrew was sad, but I was even sadder. When Mama leaned over to kiss me, I hugged her so tight she could hardly breathe. "I'll never forget you," I whispered.

Mama drew back. "What did you say?"

"Nothing," I mumbled. "I love you, Mama."

She smiled. "Well, for goodness sake, you little jacka-napes, I love you too."

Smoothing the quilt over me, she turned to the others. "What Andrew needs is a good night's sleep. In the morning, he'll be himself again, just wait and see."

"I hope so," Andrew said.

Papa frowned. "No one will get any sleep, good or bad, with Buster making such a racket. I don't know what ails that animal."

While we'd been talking, Andrew had gone to the window and whistled for the dog. Though the Tylers hadn't heard the loud two-fingered blast, Buster definitely had. His howls made the hair on my neck prickle. Even Andrew looked frightened. He backed away from the window and sat quietly in the rocker.

"Edward told me a dog howls when somebody in the family is about to die," Theo said uneasily.

Papa shook his head. "That's superstitious nonsense, Theodore. Surely you know better than to believe someone as well known for mendacity as your cousin."

Muttering to himself, Papa left the room. Taking Theo with her, Mama followed, but Hannah lingered by the bed.

I reached out and grabbed her hand. "Don't leave yet," I begged. "Stay a while."

Hannah hesitated for a moment, her face solemn, her eyes worried. "Mama's right, Andrew," she said softly. "You need to rest, you've overexcited yourself again. We've got all day tomorrow to sit in the tree and talk."

When Hannah reached up to turn off the gas jet, I glanced at Andrew. He was watching his sister from the rocker, his eyes fixed longingly on her face. A little wave of jealousy swept over me. He'd get to be with her for years, but all I had were a few more minutes.

In the darkness, Hannah smiled down at me. "Close your eyes," she said. "Go to sleep."

"But I'll never see you again."

Hannah's smile vanished. "Don't talk nonsense," she whispered. "You'll see me tomorrow and every day after that."

In the corner, Andrew stared at his sister and rocked the chair harder. In the silent room I heard it creak, saw it move back and forth.

Starled by the sound, Hannah glanced at the rocker and drew in her breath. Turning to me, she said, "Lord, the moon's making me as fanciful as you. I thought I saw —"

She shook her head. "I must need a good night's sleep

myself." Kissing me lightly on the nose, Hannah left the room without looking at the rocking chair again.

As soon as we were alone, Andrew said, "What now, Drew? Am I going to be invisible forever? A ghost they'll never see?"

Standing there in my pajamas, he looked as desperate as the night we'd met. He'd been dying of diphtheria then. Now he was cured, he was home, but things were still far from settled. I was real and he wasn't.

Fumbling from fear, I began unbuttoning the nightshirt. "Maybe if we change clothes again," I said uncertainly. "If I go up to the attic, if you stay here . . ."

Following my example, Andrew slipped out of my pajamas. When I put them on, the cloth felt scratchy and unfamiliar. I snapped the elastic waistband against my stomach, studied the rockets printed on the sleeves, went to the mirror and gazed at my reflection.

"You look like you did when I first saw you," Andrew said. "Except for your shiner."

I touched my eye and winced. "How will I explain this to Aunt Blythe?"

"That's easy enough. Tell her you walked into a door." He frowned. "It's going to be more difficult for me. How can a black eye disappear overnight?"

"Just say it's another example of your miraculous self-healing powers. Like the fever — no one ever understood how you recovered so fast from that."

Andrew leapt on the bed and bounced up and down. In midair, he crowed, "Andrew Joseph Tyler, boy wonder. Nothing can harm him, nothing can kill him. He's indestructible!"

As Andrew crashed, his mood popped like a balloon. "Oh,

Lord, Drew," he whispered, "I hope I really am indestructible. Buster's giving me the heebie-jeebies. If I'd known he was going to howl like that, I would never have whistled for him."

From somewhere behind the house, we heard Papa scolding the dog. By the time the kitchen door slammed shut, the only noise was the shrill rasping of cicadas.

In the sudden silence, Andrew grabbed my hand and shook it. "I'll miss you, Drew. You've been a regular gent."

It was hard not to cry, but I was determined to show Andrew I could be as tough as he was. "I'll miss you too," I admitted. "And Hannah and Theo and Mama and Papa. I never had a brother or a sister or a dog of my own before."

"But you won't miss Edward. He'll be there waiting for you." Andrew meant it as a joke, but neither of us laughed.

Suddenly serious, I gripped his shoulders tightly and stared into his eyes. "How will I know what happens to you?"

"Look in the graveyard," Andrew said in a melancholy voice. "If you don't see my tombstone, you'll know I didn't die."

He laughed to show me he was joking again, but death was even less funny than the old man in the wheelchair. Reaching out, Andrew crooked his little finger with mine. "If I live, I'll find a way to let you know, Drew," he promised. "I owe you that much — and a whole lot more."

After a little silence, Andrew's face brightened. "You don't suppose you could stay, do you? Just think of the fun we'd have playing tricks on Edward and Mrs. Armiger." He laughed at his own thoughts. "Why, we'd make their heads spin, Drew. They wouldn't know one of us from the other."

For a moment, it seemed possible. My mother and father were away, they wouldn't miss me. As for Aunt Blythe — well, we'd think of some way to let her know I was all right. We were bouncing on the bed, singing "Yip-I-Addy-I-Ay," when the door opened and Mama appeared. It was Andrew she looked at, not me.

"Why are you still awake?" she asked. "I told you to go to sleep."

As Mama approached the bed, Andrew flung his arms around her. "You can see me, Mama," he cried. "Oh, thank the Lord! It's me, your own true son, back again for keeps."

She stared at him, perplexed. "What nonsense is this? Of course I can see you. Of course it's you. Who else would it be, you silly goose?"

I slid off the bed and ran to her side. "Me," I shouted, "it could be me."

When Mama didn't even blink, I tugged at her nightgown. "Look at me," I begged. "I'm here too, we both are, Andrew and me. Can't you see us both?" I hugged her, but all she did was shiver.

"No wonder this room is so drafty," she murmured. "The attic door is wide open."

Andrew and I stared at each other, his face reflecting my disappointment. He was visible, I was invisible. Like the design on his quilt, the pattern had reversed.

Sadly I released Mama. As I turned away, Andrew whispered, "We'll meet again, Drew. I swear it."

Mama looked at him. "What did you say?"

"Oh, nothing." Hiding his face from his mother, Andrew winked at me and said, "I was just talking to myself, Mama."

144

I took one long last look at Andrew. Much as I wanted to stay, it was time to leave. When Mama reached out to close the attic door, I slipped through it like a ghost. The door shut behind me. I was alone at the bottom of the dark stairs with nowhere to go but home.

Chapter 22

The marbles lay on the attic floor where we'd left them, but Papa had extinguished the candle. It was just a lump of wax now, its wick too small to light again. The faint smell of smoke lingered in the still air like a long-ago birthday party.

Crawling about in the shadows, I gathered immies and carnelians, cat's-eyes and moonstones. Last of all I found the red bull's-eye. Andrew's lucky shooter had gone wide of its target and rolled into a dark corner. For a few moments, I held it between my palms, feeling its warmth. Reluctantly, I dropped it into the leather bag with the others. Click. The sound was loud in the quiet attic.

After I'd hidden Andrew's things under the floor, I felt the air thicken and darken the way it had before. My ears rang, my head ached, I was too dizzy to stand, but I wasn't frightened this time. Knowing what would happen, I closed my eyes and fell into the spinning blackness unafraid.

When I opened my eyes, I was dazzled by the bright moonlight pouring through the windows. Andrew crouched on the floor a few feet away, his face puzzled. My heart leapt at the sight of him, but when I moved closer, I realized

I'd been tricked by the huge mirror that once hung above the Tylers' parlor mantel. My own reflection stared at me, sad and alone, surrounded by things from Andrew's home — the stuffed pheasant, the parlor organ, Mama's dressmaker's dummy, the fancy hall coatrack.

But where were Mama and Papa? Where was Hannah? Theo? Andrew? Seeing their possessions abandoned and covered with dust made my heart ache. In my haste to leave, I stumbled over boxes and crates, stubbed my toe, barked my shins. Cobwebs clung to my face like shrouds. A mouse scurried over my foot.

When I reached the top of the stairs, I saw Aunt Blythe peering up at me. "Drew," she said softly, "were you walking in your sleep again?"

I put my foot on the top step and shivered. The wood was cold against my bare skin. Slowly, I went down to meet my aunt.

"Your eye," she said. "You've hurt yourself."

"The door." I touched my face. "I must have bumped into it."

"That's what woke me up — the sound of a door slamming. I thought I'd dreamed it." Aunt Blythe took my hand and led me to bed as if I were a little child.

Aching with exhaustion, I sank into a deep, dreamless sleep.

The sound of traffic woke me in the morning. When I opened my eyes, I saw checked curtains blowing in the breeze. The tumbling-block quilt covering me was old and faded. My posters hung on the walls. The horses' heads were gone.

The wallpaper had been covered over, but, looking

closely, I saw tiny roses under the blue paint. The pattern repeated itself endlessly, meeting at corners, refusing to disappear completely.

"Andrew," I whispered, "are you still here?"

The floor creaked, and I turned my head, expecting to see him in the doorway. It was my aunt.

"How do you feel this morning, Drew?"

I told her I was fine, but she insisted on checking my temperature. "I know it's silly to worry, but whenever you look the slightest bit off color I'm afraid you're getting sick again."

She stuck a thermometer in my mouth. "Diphtheria — that was the last thing anyone expected. Like most modern children, you were immunized when you were a baby. The doctors were absolutely mystified."

When my aunt was satisfied I had no fever, I said, "I don't remember much about the hospital."

"No wonder," she said. "You were out of your head most of the time. Didn't know anybody. Not even your own parents. We were afraid you had brain damage."

"I guess I wasn't myself," I said slyly.

Aunt Blythe chuckled. "That's exactly what your father said — 'Drew just isn't himself.' " She ruffled my hair. "Well, except for that shiner, you're fine now. How about getting dressed and having breakfast?"

When I sat down at the table, Great-grandfather looked up from his oatmeal and scowled. "Still here, I see," he muttered. "You've been fighting too. Just what I'd expect of a ruffian like you."

Aunt Blythe patted her father's hand. "Drew was sleep-walking again. He met a door head on, poor thing."

She turned away to pour herself another cup of coffee, and I leaned toward Great-grandfather. "I know who you think I am," I whispered, "but you're wrong. I'm Drew, not Andrew."

Great-grandfather shook his head violently. Pushing his bowl away, he wheeled himself out of the kitchen. From the back, he looked even more vulnerable — scrawny neck, big ears, thin hair. It was hard to believe he was truly Edward. No wonder Andrew hadn't recognized him.

Aunt Blythe sighed. "I'm sorry Father is so unpleasant, Drew. No matter how I try, I can't convince him you aren't his cousin Andrew. He must have truly despised that boy to be so hateful to you."

Without looking up, I ran my finger around the A carved in the table. "What happened to Andrew?"

Aunt Blythe frowned as if she were trying hard to remember. While she pondered, I held my breath. Finally, she shook her head. "I don't really know."

"The day we found his picture," I said cautiously, "you said he . . ." I paused, took a deep breath, and forced myself to finish the sentence. "You said Andrew died."

She stared at me over the rim of her cup. "I must have been confused," she said slowly. "Father had an uncle who died in childhood. His name was Andrew. Maybe I was thinking of him."

Getting to her feet, Aunt Blythe gathered the dishes and filled the sink with hot water. The sun shone through the kitchen window, bees buzzed in the hollyhocks, birds sang. Across the backyard, I saw the grove where Hannah and I had played marbles. The trees were taller now, and the family burial ground was hidden under a jungle of honeysuckle and brambles.

"Look for my grave," Andrew had said. "If you don't see it, you'll know I didn't die."

I ran out the back door and jumped off the porch the way I used to. Binky chased me across the lawn, barking joyfully. Unlike Buster, he didn't care who I was — Drew or Andrew. A boy to play with was all he wanted.

Scrambling through weeds, pushing brambles aside, burrowing under tangles of honeysuckle, I finally found Lucy's grave. On either side of it were two tall headstones. The inscriptions were worn and weather-stained. I had to scrape the moss away to read the names. Papa had died in 1919, and Mama had died twenty years later in 1939. So long ago — before I was born, before my father was born, but it made my heart ache with sadness. It was like visiting my own parents' burial place.

I plunged deeper into the weeds. On my hands and knees, I searched for a stone with Andrew's name on it. Sweat plastered my T-shirt to my back, gnats hummed in my ears, mosquitoes raised welts on my bare arms, but I was determined to search every inch of the burial ground for my friend. I had to know, had to be sure.

Hidden in the brambles, I found the final resting place of my great-great-great-grandfather, Captain Andrew Joseph Tyler. I found his wife's grave too and some of their children, including an Andrew Joseph who'd died way back in 1877. He must have been the one Aunt Blythe had mentioned, Great-grandfather's uncle, Papa's brother.

There was no other Andrew. I jumped as high as I could and shouted "Yip-I-Addy-I-Ay!" so loudly my voice echoed back to me. "We did it!" I yelled. "You didn't die, Andrew, you didn't die!"

Behind me, I heard someone laugh. Whirling around, I saw a flash of white high in the branches of the tree Hannah and I had climbed so often.

"Hannah," I cried. "Is that you?"

No one answered. Leaves shifted and shimmered in the sunlight, tricking my eyes with shadows, bushes rustled and shook. Arrowing toward me, Binky plunged out of the honeysuckle. In his mouth was an old croquet ball. He dropped it at my feet and wagged his tail.

Under the dirt and moss clinging to it, I saw a faded red stripe. Binky had found one of the balls Buster had buried so long ago. Perhaps the very one I'd once whacked into the poison ivy.

"Whuff," Binky said, "whuff." He wanted me to throw the ball, but I held it tightly.

"No," I said, "you can't have this one, old boy."

"Drew," Aunt Blythe called, "come out of those weeds. Do you want a good dose of poison ivy?"

I ran to my aunt. "Did you know there's an old family burial ground here?"

"Goodness, yes. One of these days I plan to pull the weeds, but I've had so much else to do I haven't gotten around to it yet."

"I'll help you. I don't want to forget —" I closed my mouth just in time to keep myself from saying *Mama and Papa.*

Aunt Blythe looked at me closely. "You've been in the heat too long, Drew. Just look at you, you're all tired out. Come inside and lie down for a while."

Taking my arm, she led me toward the house. Great-grandfather sat on the porch, head thrust out like a hungry bird waiting to be fed, mumbling to himself. He scowled at me but said nothing.

When she'd settled me on the living room couch, my aunt noticed the croquet ball. "Where did you find that dirty old thing?"

She reached out to take it, but I clung to it. "Let me

keep it," I said. "It reminds me, reminds me . . ." Without finishing the sentence, I closed my eyes, too weary to explain.

Aunt Blythe stroked my hair. "Of course you can keep it, Drew."

After she left, I lay still. I was in the old parlor, the very room I'd rested in once before. Although most of the Tylers' furniture was gone, the same clock ticked on the mantel. Outside, birds sang and cicadas hummed and buzzed just as they had that afternoon. Even though I couldn't see her, I was sure Mama was nearby, humming old hymns while she dusted the furniture, pausing now and then to scold Theo, calling to Hannah, ordering Buster outside. With the memory of her voice in my ears, I fell asleep.

An hour or so later, Aunt Blythe woke me. "This came for you in the mail, Drew."

I took the postcard — a night view of the Eiffel Tower sparkling with lights. On the back was a note from Mom and Dad. The work on the dig was finished, they were enjoying Paris, they'd see me soon.

Beside me, Aunt Blythe drew in her breath sharply. "Why, I never!" Waving a letter covered with spidery handwriting, she said, "What a surprise! After all these years, Hannah wants to pay me a visit. She'd love to see the house she grew up in."

At the sound of Hannah's name, my heart beat faster. Speechless with happiness, I listened to my aunt chatter excitedly.

"She says John died last winter and she's staying in Riverview to straighten out his estate." Aunt Blythe paused to scrutinize the letter. "Listen to this, Drew: 'You'll find me a bit long in the tooth, Blythe, but, never fear, I still have my wits about me. You might warn Edward I'm not a jot sweeter than I was the last time we met!' "

Aunt Blythe laughed. "In other words, Hannah hasn't changed a bit!"

"When is she coming?"

"Tomorrow afternoon." Aunt Blythe clapped her hands. "Oh, I can't wait to see her!"

"Me either!"

Aunt Blythe smiled. "Fancy your being so pleased. I didn't think you'd be interested in an old lady like Hannah."

Old? I stared at my aunt. I'd seen Hannah less than twenty-four hours ago — dark hair piled on her head, laughing, teasing, challenging me to a game of marbles or a race to the top of a tree.

Beside me, Aunt Blythe sighed. "Well, Hannah won't find *me* a kid, will she?" Getting to her feet, she smiled at me. "Rest a little longer if you like. Lunch will be ready in about fifteen minutes."

Alone in the living room, I studied the flowered wallpaper, searching for the young girl's face I'd once seen in the roses. Yes, she was still there, but faded and dim, much harder to find than the day Mama had made me rest on the parlor sofa. Looking at her, I remembered a famous drawing my father had once shown me. "Look closely," he'd said. "Tell me what you see."

"An ugly old woman with a big nose."

"Is that all?" Dad asked.

Like magic, the lines shifted. The old woman's nose became a young girl's profile, her eye became the girl's ear, her chin the girl's throat. Two images in the same space, wavering back and forth, changing from old to young and back again, fooling your eyes. An optical illusion,

Dad said, proof there was more than one way to look at things.

But no matter how hard I tried, I couldn't see the old woman in Hannah's face any more than I could see the boy in Great-grandfather's face. I didn't want to. Surely Hannah would step out of the past unchanged, as young and beautiful as ever.

Chapter 23

The next afternoon, Aunt Blythe and I sat on the front porch waiting for Hannah. It was a hot August day, loud with the hum and drone of insects. Sunlight bounced off the windshields of cars on the highway. Every time one slowed down, I held my breath, expecting to see an old Model T chug up the driveway to the house.

"I hope Father sleeps right through Hannah's visit," Aunt Blythe said. "There's no telling what he'd say or do. At his age, too much excitement is bad for the heart."

I glanced at my aunt. She was gazing at the fields across the highway, smiling to herself. "I'll never forget the day Hannah and Father got into an argument about President Roosevelt. She was an ardent Democrat and Father — well, you can imagine. He must have been the stodgiest Republican ever born. They went at politics hammer and tongs."

Just then a big blue Buick slowed to turn into the driveway. "That must be Hannah now," Aunt Blythe said.

There were two people in the car. An old man was behind the wheel and an even older woman was sitting beside him.

"No," I said, "that's not her. It can't be."

But Aunt Blythe wasn't listening. She was hurrying toward the Buick, waving.

Speechless, I watched the man open the driver's door and get out. The sun shone on his white hair and bent back.

Aunt Blythe was helping the old woman. "Hannah," she cried, "I'm so happy to see you."

While the women embraced, the man hobbled toward me. The hand clasping the cane was roped with veins, the eyes were deepset and hooded, but clear and bright. He stopped a few feet away and smiled.

"Hello, Drew," he said. "I told you we'd meet again."

Before I could say a word, the old woman joined us. She wore a pale-gray dress. White hair slipped out of her top-knot, her shoulders curved under the weight of years. Clutching Aunt Blythe's arm with a clawlike hand, she said, "I don't believe you've met my brother Andrew. I should have told you he was coming, but he insisted on surprising you."

When she smiled, I saw the young girl in the old woman's face. It was Hannah after all, really and truly Hannah. Not the way I remembered her, not even the way I wanted her to be, but still alive, still laughing.

"This is my great-nephew Drew," Aunt Blythe said.

Seizing my hands, Hannah said, "I would have recognized him anywhere." Turning to her brother, she added, "He's the spitting image of you when you were his age."

"Indeed he is." From under bushy white eyebrows, Andrew winked at me. "Except for one thing — I never had a shiner as magnificent as the one he's sporting."

Hannah peered at my eye. Turning to her brother, she said, "My word, Andrew, have you forgotten? Edward once gave you a shiner every bit as impressive as that." She shot her brother one of the teasing looks I remembered so well.

"The odd thing was it vanished overnight. Maybe that's why you don't remember."

Aunt Blythe looked from one to the other, but it was clear she didn't understand why Hannah and Andrew were laughing. "Would you like to come inside?" she asked. "I've made lemonade and cookies."

"You two go on." Andrew rested his hand on my shoulder. "I'd like to borrow my young cousin for a few minutes. We'll join you later."

I watched Aunt Blythe help Hannah up the stairs. "She moves a mite slower now," Andrew said, "and so do I."

Keeping his hand on my shoulder to steady himself, he walked across the grass. We'd only gone a few steps when Binky tore around the side of the house, barking and growling at the sight of a stranger.

"Binky!" I yelled.

I needn't have worried. Andrew held out his hand and called the dog's name. Immediately, Binky hushed. Wagging his tail, he jumped up to lick his friend's nose.

"You remember me, don't you, fellow?" Andrew scratched Binky behind his ears. "No matter how old a body gets, I reckon you smell the same to a dog."

In the backyard, Andrew and I sat down in a pair of wooden lawn chairs. Binky lay beside us and rested his nose on Andrew's shoes. For a while, neither of us spoke. The day that stretched between us had turned into a lifetime for my old friend.

Andrew lit his pipe, took a few puffs, and sighed contentedly. "I don't know how to thank you for the time you gave me, Drew. The life I've had, the things I've seen and done. If it hadn't been for you, I'd be pushing up the weeds over there with Mama and Papa and Lucy."

For a moment we contemplated the tangled vines and brambles hiding the tombstones. "The first thing I did yesterday was look for your grave," I said. "I sure was glad not to find it."

"You couldn't be a jot gladder than I am." Andrew smiled and blew a smoke ring. We watched it float away, round and perfect against the blue sky.

Leaning closer, he said, "I must admit you had a good influence on me, Drew. Mama always thought the fever sweetened me up, but I know it was you. Not that I turned into a danged sissy or anything like that. Just got a little less prickly."

He chuckled and patted my knee. "I hope you got some of the pepper I lost. As I recall, you sorely needed it."

"When I jumped off the trestle, I felt like you," I admitted. "I'm still not sure who hit Edward — you or me. But I do know one thing. There's this boy named Martin back in Chicago. All my life he's been picking on me. The next time he tries anything, he sure is going to be surprised." Grinning at Andrew, I raised my fists and boxed the air between us.

"Now, now," he said, "Let's not get carried away, Drew. You don't want to be as cocky as I used to be."

At that moment, the back door opened, and Great-grandfather wheeled himself outside. Slowly and carefully, Hannah stepped through the door behind him. Aunt Blythe followed, balancing a tray loaded with a pitcher of lemonade and five glasses.

"Come along, you two," Hannah called.

"Tarnation," Andrew muttered. "Am I going to have to see that jackass today?" Without letting me help, he levered himself out of the chair with his cane. "I bet Hannah woke the old coot up just to make me miserable."

When we joined the others on the porch, Great-grandfather refused to look at us. Keeping his head down, he fidgeted with the blanket on his lap.

"This is a fine way to greet me," Andrew said.

"Maybe he doesn't recognize you." Aunt Blythe bent down to peer into Great-grandfather's face. "Your cousins are here, Father. Can you say hello to Hannah and Andrew?"

"It's my house," he mumbled. "They can't have it."

Andrew looked as if he wanted to give his cousin a punch in the nose, but Hannah intervened. "We know the house is yours, Edward," she said. "Don't worry, we haven't come to take it back. Andrew and I have our own home."

Great-grandfather raised his head and stared at Hannah. "You never liked me. Neither did your brothers. I wasn't welcome in this house when you lived here. Now it's mine and *you're* not welcome."

Ignoring Aunt Blythe's protests, Great-grandfather wheeled himself toward the back door. "You and your Roosevelt," he muttered before he disappeared. "Too bad you women ever got the vote."

"Please excuse Father," Aunt Blythe said. "He's having one of his bad days."

Andrew snorted. "All of Edward's days have been bad, every blasted one of them."

Hannah rapped his fingers. "Don't be so ornery, Andrew. What will Blythe think of you?"

"I say what's on my mind. Always have." Andrew shot me a grin. "Isn't that right, Drew?"

Hannah frowned at her brother. "How on earth can Drew answer a question like that?"

My aunt didn't notice the warning tone in her cousin's voice, but I did. From the look she gave Andrew, I was sure Hannah knew everything.

To break the tension, Aunt Blythe smiled at Andrew. "Hannah tells me you're an archeologist," she said. "Drew's father has followed in your footsteps. He spent the whole summer in France, excavating a Roman ruin."

A spark of mischief flared in Andrew's eyes. "Why, it could be the other way around," he said. "Perhaps I got the idea from *him*."

Hannah gave Andrew a sharp poke with her cane. Luckily, Aunt Blythe didn't notice that either.

"You have the oddest sense of humor," she said to Andrew. "It's a pity you spent most of your life overseas. I'm sure I would have enjoyed knowing you."

To escape his sister's reach, Andrew shifted his position. "It's strange," he said to my aunt, "but I feel like I *do* know you."

"Isn't that funny?" Aunt Blythe stared at him. "Even though I've never set eyes on you before, I feel the same way."

With a little guidance from Hannah, the conversation changed to Andrew's years in South America. For at least an hour he entertained us with his adventures, which Hannah claimed were highly exaggerated.

"He never tells a story the same way twice," she told me. "You wouldn't believe how much more exciting they've gotten since the first time I heard them."

"You didn't marry?" Aunt Blythe asked Andrew.

He glanced at me. "When I was a boy no older than Drew, I had a close brush with death. It always seemed to me a miracle that I lived."

Once more Hannah made an attempt to stop her brother with a poke of her cane, but Andrew went on talking, his eyes on my face, his voice solemn. "I often thought I'd been meant to die, so I decided to lead a solitary life. There's no way of telling what one person might do to change the history of the world."

Before he could say anything else, Hannah patted Aunt Blythe's arm. "I brought along an old photo album. Would you please fetch it from the car?"

As soon as my aunt was out of sight, Hannah said, "If you don't hush, Andrew, we're going to leave the minute Blythe comes back. I swear I don't know what ails you. You might as well be twelve years old!"

She turned to me then and took my hand. "You know what I'm talking about, don't you, Drew? He was an absolute imp when he was your age and he still is. All that's changed is his outside."

I stared into Hannah's eyes, faded now to the color of shadows on winter snow. "He told you, didn't he?"

"In some ways, I think I knew all along." Hannah squeezed my hand. "I'm so glad we've lived long enough to see you again."

I flung my arms around her. She felt as thin-boned as a bird, and I was afraid to hug her too tightly. I didn't want to hurt her.

"It must be a shock to see us so old," Hannah said. "I'm afraid I couldn't climb a tree or shoot a marble if my life depended on it. Neither could Andrew, but I doubt he'll admit it."

"If I put my mind to it," Andrew said, "I could beat Drew with one hand tied behind my back. He was never any match for me."

Hannah raised her eyebrows. "It seems to me he outplayed you once."

"Pshaw. What's one game?"

If Aunt Blythe hadn't come back just then, I'd have argued, maybe even challenged Andrew to a rematch, but instead, I smiled and leaned my head against Hannah's shoulder, happy to feel her arm around me. This close, she still smelled like rose water.

Turning the pages of the album, Hannah showed us pictures of Mama and Papa, Theo, herself — and Andrew.

"These are my favorites." She pointed to the photographs John had taken of us in the Model T. We were all smiling except Theo. He sat beside me, scowling into the camera, still angry about Mrs. Armiger and the music lessons.

"We wanted Theo to come with us today," Hannah said, "but he's living down in Florida with his third wife — a lady half his age, I might add."

Andrew nudged me. "He sends his best, said he hopes to see you again someday."

I glanced at Aunt Blythe but she was staring at the photograph. "The resemblance is incredible. If I didn't know better, I'd swear it was Drew."

Andrew chuckled. "Take a good look at me now. This is how the poor boy will look when he's ninety-six."

I studied his rosy face, his white hair and mustache. His back was bent, but his eyes sparkled with mischief. Going to his side, I put my arms around him. "You're not so bad," I said. Dropping my voice to a whisper, I added, "I wouldn't be surprised if you could still beat me in a game of ringer."

Chapter 24

Long before I was ready to say good-bye, Hannah rose to her feet and beckoned to Andrew. "We've had enough excitement for one day. It's time to leave."

After making sure Aunt Blythe wasn't looking, Andrew pulled a leather bag out of his pocket. "She thinks you already have these," he said. "They're yours for keeps now."

I clasped the marbles to my heart and stared at him through a blur of tears. "Come back soon, Andrew."

He hugged me so hard he squashed my nose against his bony shoulder. "At my age, I can't promise anything, but I'll do my best to see you again, and that's the truth. After all, Hannah and I aren't that far away. With modern cars and highways, Riverview's a sight closer than it used to be."

Reluctant to let him go, I looked him in the eye. "No matter what happens, I'll always keep you here." I struck my chest with my fist. "Right here in my heart as long as I live."

Andrew smiled. "I fancy you picked up that pretty notion from Hannah." Hugging me again, he said, "I hope your heart lasts as long as mine has, Drew. I want you to have all the time in the world to do whatever you like."

I watched him help Hannah into the car and then position himself behind the steering wheel. While Aunt Blythe and I waved good-bye, the big Buick bumped down the driveway, turned right, and vanished in the direction of Riverview.

Aunty Blythe went inside to check on Great-grandfather, but I sat on the front steps and watched the sun sink behind the trees across the highway. A little chill crept across my skin. Summer was almost over. Soon my parents would return and I'd go back to Chicago. There would be no more midnight meetings in the attic. No croquet games with Hannah, no boxing lessons from John, no fights with Edward.

Behind me, the door opened, and I heard the wheelchair squeak as it rolled through. "Haven't changed a bit, either one of them," Great-grandfather muttered. "Coming around here, showing off, laughing like the world's their oyster."

When I turned to face him, Great-grandfather scowled. "What the Sam Hill are you doing here? I thought Hannah took you with her. How long am I going to have to put up with the sight of your ugly face?"

Aunt Blythe looked at me and sighed apologetically. Her eyes said, "What's the use?"

Great-grandfather wasn't paying attention to either one of us. He stared fixedly at the lawn, his eyes moving back and forth as if he were watching something only he could see. For a moment, I thought I heard laughter, the click of one croquet ball striking another, a dog barking.

I stared at the empty yard, trying hard to see what Great-grandfather saw, but nothing shifted, nothing changed. If the Tylers were playing croquet, they were visible to him and him alone. The only dog in sight was Binky. Running across the lawn to meet him, I took the stick he carried and threw it as hard as I could. It sailed across the sky, and Binky dashed after it.

As the dog disappeared into the bushes, I looked up at the attic window and remembered the flash of white I'd seen the day I arrived — my first glimpse of Andrew. Funny to think I'd been scared. Nothing stirred in the attic now. No one watched, no one waited.

Deep in my pocket, I touched the red bull's-eye, warm as blood and twice as lucky. The marbles were mine for keeps. They were safe, and so was Andrew.

° HOW TO PLAY RINGER °

1. Draw a circle at least three feet in diameter on a smooth, flat surface.
2. In the center, draw a cross. Lay thirteen marbles on it: one in the middle and three on each arm. These are the targets, sometimes called ducks or miggles.
3. To determine who gets the first turn, you must lag. Draw two lines about a foot apart. One is the lag line; the other is the back line. Step back ten paces and draw a pitching line. From here, use an underhanded throw to roll your shooter at the lag line. The player whose marble lands closest goes first. If your marble stops on the lag line, you win automatically, but if it crosses the back line, you lose automatically.

   Note: In ringer, the first player has a distinct advantage. To win, you must knock seven marbles out of the circle. A good player can do this on his first try.
4. The first player kneels outside the ring and knuckles down to shoot. You must keep at least one knuckle on the ground, and you must not move your hand, an offense called "whisting."
5. If no marbles leave the circle, you lose your turn. If

your shooter is still in the ring, leave it there. That's where you shoot from next time. If it rolls outside, you can shoot from anywhere on the ring's perimeter.

Note: Your opponent may knock your shooter out of the ring. If he does, you shoot from the place your marble lands.

6. If you shoot one or more marbles out of the ring, you can try again, provided your shooter stays *inside* the ring. If your shooter rolls outside with the other marbles, you keep the ones you hit, but you lose your turn.

7. To keep your turn, shoot from the place where your shooter stopped.

8. The first player to knock seven marbles out of the ring wins the game.

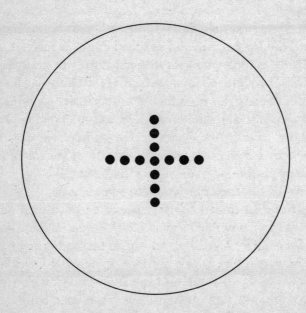